THE EXPERIMENT

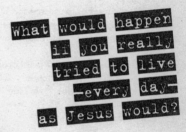

What would happen if you really tried to live —every day— as Jesus would?

TODD TEMPLE

ZondervanPublishingHouse
Grand Rapids, Michigan

A Division of HarperCollinsPublishers

The Experiment
Copyright © 1998 by Todd Temple

Requests for information should be addressed to:
🏰 ZondervanPublishingHouse
Grand Rapids, Michigan 49530

Library of Congress Cataloging-in-Publication Data

Temple, Todd, 1958-
    The experiment / Todd Temple.
        p.   cm.
      Summary: For extra credit in World Religions class
two teenagers agree to participate in an experiment in
which they attempt to live for two weeks exactly as Jesus
would.
    ISBN: 0-310-22348-2 (softcover)
    [1. High schools—Fiction. 2. Schools—Fiction. 3.
Christian life—Fiction.] I. Title.
PZ7.T2535Ex 1998
[Fic]—dc21   98–10311
                                       CIP
                                       AC

All Scripture quotations, unless otherwise indicated, are taken from
the *Holy Bible: New International Version*®. NIV®. Copyright ©
1973, 1978, 1984 by International Bible Society. Used by permission
of Zondervan Publishing House. All rights reserved.

Published in association with the literary agency of Alive
Communications, Inc., 1465 Kelly Johnson Blvd #320, Colorado
Springs, CO 80920.

Interior design by Sue Vandenberg Koppenol

Printed in the United States of America

---

98 99 00 01 02 03 04 /✤ OP/ 10 9 8 7 6 5 4 3 2

To Tom Julian,
who first showed me what Jesus would do

Contents

1

The Experiment

"Hey, anybody home?"

Tina Lockhart looked up to see her friend Camille settling into the next desk. She almost groaned. She had purposely arrived at her World Religions class early so that she'd have some undisturbed time to study her script for the church musical.

Camille looked down at the script on Tina's desk and blurted out, "Oh, yeah—that's on Sunday, right?"

"Yep. Day after tomorrow. And I've got the lead role—and lots to memorize still." Tina turned back to her lines, allowing her long blond hair to fall like a privacy curtain between her and her classmate.

Camille got out her notebook, fussed with some papers, then interrupted again. "So, Tina, are you excited about today?"

"Why?" This time she didn't look up.

"You know—today we start the chapter on Christianity. Your favorite subject!"

"Oh, yeah. I forgot. Speaking of which, I've really got to concentrate on this right now."

"Sorry." Camille got the hint, but too late. The tardy bell rang, and as Ms. Veras made her way to the

front of the class, Tina put away the script and glared
at her friend. Camille shrugged apologetically.

After checking the roll, Ms. Veras launched into
her explanation of how their study of the Christian
religion would proceed, but Tina barely listened.
She knew the routine. They would study Christianity for two weeks, with a quiz at the end of each
week—the same pattern they had followed in their
examination of Buddhism, Hinduism, and Judaism.

"In this country," Ms. Veras began, "Christianity is as American as apple pie and baseball.
Many people see it like a Norman Rockwell painting: a big white church with a cross on the steeple.
Friendly people dressed in their Sunday best are fil-
ing out the doors to smile and shake the minister's
hand, while rosy-cheeked boys and girls play on the
front lawn, trying not to soil their shiny black shoes.
It's a warm and friendly picture. But history paints
a portrait of Christianity that's not so cheerful."

Tina knew what was coming next. Ms. Veras
reminded her of an afternoon TV talk-show host.
She would start out warm and cuddly, then say
something controversial to spark a response. This
time, Ms. Veras recited a long history of evils committed in the name of Christ: the Crusades, the
Inquisition, witch hunts, slavery, Northern Ireland,
Bosnia, on and on. She had quite a list.

Then she turned it over to the class. "So now
we've got two pictures: that Norman Rockwell-like

painting, and a blood-stained picture from history. What's *your* picture of Christianity? What does this religion look like to you—good and bad?"

Tina looked across the room. A few students—the ones she knew from church or the campus Christian club—gave her the look she had come to expect. It meant *Say something.* They did that whenever they felt persecuted, which happened a lot in Veras's class. Tina was proud that her many classroom stands for the faith had earned her a reputation as an outspoken Christian. Still, she decided to hold her tongue. *Let them squirm,* she thought. *We'll set the record straight in a minute.*

After a few long seconds of silence, someone raised a hand. "I don't mean this as an offense to Christians, but it seems like, sometimes, they act like they're trying to control people's lives."

Then another hand: "Some Christians seem to think that they've got a special deal with God—that they're the only ones who get to go to heaven."

Well—that's true, Tina thought. But she said nothing.

More hands went up. "I know Christians who go to parties and get drunk on Saturday night, then get all dressed up and go to church on Sunday morning. They're like two different people."

"Hypocrites," someone murmured in reply.

Tina felt her face get hot. She was just about to say something when Camille spoke up. "Christians aren't perfect. No one is. But they do a lot of good stuff too. They help the homeless, and run shelters—and missionaries go to other countries to help poor people."

Tina was pleased that someone besides herself had spoken up for their faith—although she wondered why Camille had said *they* instead of *we*. Other students joined in now, saying good things about Christianity—including a few students that Tina hadn't realized were Christians. All in all, they put together a pretty good defense.

Then Victoria jumped into the discussion: "Yeah, okay—they do lots of good stuff for society, but what about how they treat women? Some of them say that the man is the head of the family, and they don't let women become ministers. And what about those fanatics who blow up abortion clinics and say that God told them to do it?"

Tina shot up her hand.

Ms. Veras turned to her. "Tina, I was wondering when we'd hear from you."

A few students snickered, which made Tina's face burn hotter. She took a breath, then said, "You can't blame Christianity for the problems Christians cause. It just means that they're not really acting like Christ." It came out a little louder, a little more agitated than she had planned, but she felt reassured when she glanced at Camille, who mouthed a secret *Amen!*

"You're right, Tina," Ms. Veras replied, "but whose fault is that? Christians claim that Christ was perfect. If he was, he set an impossible standard. How can anyone possibly act just like him? Do *you* act just like him?"

Tina felt every eye in the room focus on her. Somehow, the discussion had turned from "Christianity" to "Tina's behavior," and Tina didn't like it one bit. Sounding not as bold as before, she said, "Well, no—I don't. But I try. Before I make a decision I try to ask myself, 'What would Jesus do if he were in my situation?'"

A twinge of guilt. The truth was, the idea of asking herself, "What would Jesus do?" had never occurred to her before last Wednesday night, when her church youth pastor had talked about that idea at their weekly Bible study. She half-opened her mouth to amend her statement, then thought better of it and kept silent.

Ms. Veras took a few steps toward Tina's desk. "But how can you guess what Jesus would do? For one thing, he was a *man*. He lived two thousand years ago, in a totally different culture. And if that's not enough, everything you know about him, I assume, comes from the Bible—and who knows if that story is even accurate?"

"I believe in the Bible!" Tina shot back, then paused to lower her voice. "And I believe that what it says about Jesus is true." She paused again, trying to recall the verse Pastor Jim taught on. "It says that Jesus is our example and that we're supposed to follow in his steps. That means playing Follow the Leader—doing what he would do." Again she felt guilty, this time for not paying more attention to Jim.

"I want to believe you, Tina," said Ms. Veras, turning now and walking slowly back toward the front of the room as she talked, "but I still think that Jesus' example, as you have described it, is impossible to live up to. Even if you could figure out what Jesus would do today if he were in your shoes, you would still have to remember to stop every moment and ask, 'What would Jesus do?'—always second-guessing the right answer, and all the time knowing that you can't live up to his perfect standard. I think that if you really followed this standard, your life would be miserable."

Throughout the semester, Tina had grown accustomed to her teacher's snips at Christianity. She could handle that. But now Veras was attacking her *personal* faith—and doing it in front of the whole class. Tina didn't know whether to cry or just tell Veras to shut up and mind her own business. But to her surprise, when she opened her mouth, what she said was,

"I admit that being a Christian isn't easy, but it's not impossible. And it *doesn't* make me miserable. Maybe that's because I don't always remember to try to do what Jesus would do, but I think if I did, my life would be *better*, not worse. And to prove it to you, I'll do what I said I should do. For the next two weeks, I'll make my daily decisions according to what I think Jesus would do. Then you can decide for yourself if I'm miserable or not."

"But how will I know if you're really doing it?"

"Ask me. And if I lie, then I'm a big fat hypocrite anyway, so you'll have proved your point." A few of her classmates laughed—and the sense of relief that washed through the room told Tina just how tense the confrontation had actually become.

Ms. Veras turned slowly, smiled slyly—and Tina had the odd feeling that she'd just fallen into some kind of trap. "OK, Tina. You're on. Consider it an extra credit project. Two weeks from today, why don't you give us a report of your 'experiment'—call it 'What happens when you really do what Jesus would do.' And to make it fair, let's offer it to the rest of the class. Anyone willing to join Tina in this little experiment? Some of you could use the extra credit!"

To Tina's surprise, not one of the other Christians raised a hand. She glared at Camille, but Camille wouldn't look at her. Tina almost reached over to tap her.

"No one else wants extra credit? Last chance. Going once ... going twice ..."

Tina saw a hand go up in the back of the room. That sloppy Asian kid who never spoke up in class.

"Well, Tina, it looks like you're *not* alone. Mr. Chen will be joining you. Our two *guinea pigs*, Matthew and Tina, will provide the grand finale to our study of the Christian religion, each giving us an oral report of their two-week experience in doing what Jesus would do. There's the bell. See you on Monday."

As the students scrambled for the door, Ms. Veras called out, "Remember, Tina—and Matthew—Jesus works on weekends too."

2

No Big Deal

Camille escaped from class in a hurry. When Tina caught up with her, she was stuffing books into her locker.

"Some friend *you* are!"

"What do you mean?" asked Camille, a bit too innocently.

"You *know* what I mean," replied Tina, cutting through the charade. "Why didn't you volunteer for that Jesus experiment?"

"I'm getting an A in the class already. Why would I want extra credit?"

"*I* don't need the credit either! That's not the point. This is a chance to take a stand for our faith, in front of Veras and all those other people who make fun of Christians."

Camille pulled her sweater out of her locker and gave Tina a mildly scolding look. "Just because Veras asks tough questions sometimes doesn't mean she's making fun of us. And if the class laughs at her jokes, it doesn't mean they're laughing at Christianity. She *is* pretty funny sometimes. But what are you saying? Just because I didn't volunteer for the assignment, that means I'm not a Christian?" Camille slammed her locker shut.

Tina took it down a notch. "Come on. You know I'm not saying that. It's just that—well, it seems like a good opportunity to witness."

"Look, Tina—I'm really glad that you're willing to try it. But think about what you've just promised to do. Before making *any* decision, you're supposed to ask, 'What would Jesus do?'—and then do it."

"I know that. So what's wrong with that?"

"Think about it: *Every* decision! *Every* time you open your mouth, or do anything at all! You'll spend the whole day asking that question!"

"Camille, you make it sound like—listen, it takes half a second to think the question. It's no big deal."

"But it *is,* Tina. First, you've got to *remember* to ask the question. A moment ago, right before you spoke to me, did you remember to ask, What would Jesus do if he were about to speak to Camille?

"Yes—well, no. I didn't. But I'm just getting started. I only got the assignment, like, two minutes ago!"

Camille smiled. "Okay, I'll let you off the hook. But I still think it's pretty hard to remember that question all the time. Besides, how will you really know if you're really doing what Jesus would *really* do?"

"Now you're *ree-lee* starting to sound like Meez Bay-rhas." Tina mimicked their teacher's Latin accent and manner as she said it, pulling her hair back into the teacher's trademark bun and standing with a tall forward lean. It was a pretty good impression, making both of them laugh.

"I'm sorry," Camille continued, "but in a way, she was right. How can you know what Jesus would do in your shoes?"

"Because I've been a Christian almost all my life. I read my Bible, I have Christian parents, I go to a good church, and I have good Christian friends. I *know* when I'm doing what Jesus would do, because—well—it feels right. And when I'm not doing it, I feel guilty. Isn't that what it means to be a good Christian?"

Camille raised an eyebrow uncertainly, but said nothing. That didn't surprise Tina; she often seemed to be a step or two ahead of her friends spiritually, saying things that made them think. So she gave Camille a moment to ponder this latest bit of wisdom, then continued: "And best of all, now I get to explain Christianity to the rest of the class, and get extra credit besides. You missed your chance!"

"Well, you make it sound pretty easy, but still, I don't know. I don't think I'm up to that kind of commitment. Anyway, I'm glad you spoke up again today, and I wish you luck."

"Jesus wouldn't say that. He'd say, 'I'll pray for you.'

As they parted, Camille shot back, "Yes, but would he have *corrected* me for saying it?"

Now it was Tina's turn to ponder.

3

Revealed

Driving into the Lakeview Church parking lot that afternoon, Tina saw the banner flapping in the breeze: "YOUTH MUSICAL, SUNDAY 7 PM." Butterflies took flight in her stomach. She and the other members of the cast had been rehearsing for weeks, but only now was she starting to feel the excitement of it all.

Inside, her youth pastor, Jim, and the church music director assembled the cast, all members of the youth group, for a full run-through of the musical without stopping.

Backstage, she spotted Mitch, one of her classmates in Ms. Veras's class and a minor cast member in the play. She thought of asking him why he hadn't volunteered for the experiment, but in a way she was glad he hadn't. Mitch was a nerdy sophomore guy—not someone she and the other leading members in the youth group cared to hang out with.

Tina made it through the whole rehearsal without speaking to Mitch—or anyone else—about her new assignment. But afterward, as Tina and her friends were raiding the church kitchen's giant refrigerator for cold drinks, Mitch tracked her down. "Good job today in class! You really stood up for the faith!"

Amanda pulled her head out of the fridge. "What'd you do, Tina?" Tina could hear a touch of sarcasm in her friend's voice—Amanda's way of teasing her in front of someone they both thought was a loser.

"Nothing, Amanda," Tina said, trying to shut down the conversation before it started. "I'll tell you about it later." Then she grabbed the sheet of cookies from Amanda's arms and slid it onto the polished metal counter in the center of the kitchen. The half dozen students, mostly juniors and seniors, surrounded the counter like coyotes stalking their prey. In seconds, the plastic wrap was torn from the tray and peanut butter cookies were being snatched up by the handful.

Mitch didn't take the bait. *"Nothing?"* he shouted, a little too loud. Then, since he had everyone's attention, he told them all about today's World Religions class—and he made it a colorful tale, much to Tina's embarrassment. "And by the way," he concluded, "that Bible verse you referred to in class—the one Jim taught on—it's 2 Peter 2:21. I've got it right here." Mitch flipped through his ever-handy Bible.

The cookie munchers waited patiently as Mitch looked it up. Tina gave her best friend a desperate look: *Do something!*

"Here it is," Mitch continued, then read in his serious voice: "To this you were called, because

Christ suffered for you, leaving you an example, that you should follow in his steps."

When he closed the Bible, a few of the students nodded silently in agreement while the rest of them grabbed for more cookies.

"So, Mitch," Amanda said, trying to distract him, "did *you* agree to do the experiment too?"

"I wanted to, but I kind of chickened out. Ms. Veras scares me."

Someone asked, "So was Tina the only one?"

"No, Matt Chen volunteered."

"Who's *he*?" asked someone else.

"That guy who hangs out with the Antees. You know—long straggly black hair, wears that big dirty army jacket all the time."

"That's helpful, *Mitchell*," Amanda replied. "You've just described half the Antees!"

"He's the *Chinese* one," someone volunteered.

"Ohhh," Amanda said thoughtfully. "I think I know who he is. He's a freak—like *all* the Antees!"

"My, what a sweet thing to say about people Jesus died for," said Mitch. "Just because they're different, it doesn't make them freaks." Tina was surprised. That was pretty bold talk for Mitch— especially to Amanda, who loved to put him in his place.

"Save us the sermon, Mitchell," Amanda replied. "Admit it—they're pretty strange. Doing their little protest things, causing trouble, acting like they're saving the world. So Tina, do you have to work with *him* in this experiment?"

"No way!" Tina exclaimed, her mouth full of cookie.

"I don't see how she could work with him anyway," Mitch exclaimed. "He told me he's an atheist."

Amanda shook her head. "You're kidding? You *talked* to him?"

"Yeah, we used to play Little League together. He's a pretty nice guy when you get to know him. I invited him to church one time. That's when he told me he was an atheist."

Now Tina was intrigued. "What's he doing volunteering for this experiment? How can he do what Jesus would do if he's not even a *Christian*?"

Danny, who had walked into the kitchen a minute earlier, put his arm around Tina and said, "Good question. Why don't you *ask* him?"

"No way!" Tina shouted, giving her boyfriend a loving elbow jab to the rib cage.

"If you want," offered Mitch, "I can ask him on Monday." Obviously, he'd missed Danny's sarcasm.

"Don't you dare, Mitch!" Tina hissed, stepping toward him. When Danny pulled her back to his chest, she added, "If he wants to make a fool of himself with this experiment, that's his business."

Jim rushed into the kitchen just then, glancing around as he looked for something—and stopped dead. "Hey!" he yelled. "Stop raiding the preschoolers' snacks! You're taking animal crackers from the mouth of a baby! OK, everybody out!" As they filed slowly out, Jim added, "Danny, Mitch—grab a few others and come with me. We need to move some of the stage backdrops."

"So, Tina," Amanda said as they walked back to the senior high room to get their coats. "This experiment sounds like a big deal. Why didn't you tell me about it earlier?"

"I would have—if it *were* a big deal. Mitch made too big a thing out of it."

"I still don't get it," said Amanda. "What exactly do you have to *do*?"

"It's simple. For two weeks, I'm supposed to ask, 'What would Jesus do?' before I make a decision, and then do it."

"Sounds like a lot of work."

"Everyone keeps saying that!" Tina yelled. "But it's not! I'm a good Christian, right? Which means I'm kind of already doing that. If someone offers me drugs, I say no. Because that's what Jesus would do. If someone asks me to lie for them, I say no. Because that's what Jesus would do. So basically, I get to do what I've already been doing— only this time I get to tell the whole class about how great it is to be a Christian, *and* I get extra credit for doing it!"

"Hey, don't forget the part about being my best friend."

Tina gave her friend a curious look. "What do you mean?"

"You know—if someone asks you who your best friend is, you say, 'Amanda!' Because ..."

Tina picked up her meaning. "Because ... that's what Jesus would do!"

"You got it!" They laughed and gave each other a hug.

When Tina found Danny, he said, "Wanna go back to my house and watch some TV?"

"You sure you're parents won't mind?" Tina knew Danny's parents loved her almost as much as he did, but she liked to hear him say it.

"Let's not go through *that* again! Besides, they're at a party and won't be back till late."

4

Looking for Jesus

After school, Matt had taken the bus downtown to work his shift at the record store. It was an easy job, not a lot of customers, with plenty of time to listen to music. And think. Today, he was thinking of the assignment he had volunteered for in World Religions. He'd volunteered for one reason only: he *had* to. He still felt the sting of last night's argument with his dad, which had started when his dad saw his latest progress report and had ended with an ultimatum: "Either buckle down and show me a B average, or quit your job, spend your afternoons doing homework—and say goodbye to those strange friends of yours."

With only four weeks left in the semester, Matt had a lot of work to do. In most of his classes, his grade hovered somewhere between a C and a B. World Religions was his biggest problem. In Ms. Veras's class, participation in the discussions counted for one-fourth of the grade. But as the youngest student in a room of mostly juniors and seniors, and unsupported by any of his friends, he felt too intimidated to speak up.

In fact, until today, he had sat in class each afternoon saying nothing and regretting that he had ever signed up. He *could* have taken something else, too; World Religions was an elective—which explained why, as a sophomore, he was in the minority. His original reasons for taking the class seemed stupid now. First, there was Ms. Veras. She had seemed like a really cool teacher, attending some of the protest meetings his friends had staged at lunch hour. Veras didn't act like part of the "establishment"—she seemed more like an advocate, someone who wasn't afraid to speak out. Kind of like Matt himself . . . except for the speaking-out part.

But more than that, it was his atheism that had prompted him to sign up. In a class all about "God," he could stand out as the guy who didn't believe in God. It appealed to the way he pictured himself: Matt the Rebel. That looked good in theory, but when the semester had begun, it hadn't taken him long to realize that his atheism was—well—no big deal. The class was all about *religions*—who had started them, what had happened in their history, and what those religions looked like today. "God" had a very minor role in class discussions, and sometimes his name wouldn't come up for days at a time.

With few opportunities and little courage to speak out on the God nonsense, Matt saved his atheism speeches for the papers he wrote. At least Ms. Veras would read them. But that didn't work either. The teacher gave very specific topics for the papers, so he had to wander way off the point to get to his own agenda. He had turned in papers that pointed out the stupidity of each religion and every god, but they always came back with low grades, covered with Ms. Veras's red-inked comments—"Digression." "Off the track." "Doesn't answer the question."

Then came today. Matt had quickly seen that this "experiment" was the green light to say what he wanted to say. The assignment was simple: All he had to do was ask a simple question before each decision: "What would Jesus do?" Ms. Veras herself had pointed out the stupidity of that question. How could *anyone* know what an ancient, mythical character would do today? It was all subject to interpretation. All Matt had to do was read the Christian fables and make sure that his behavior was somewhat in keeping with the Jesus character.

And how tough could that be? All religious fables carried the same basic moral messages: be nice, don't lie, don't cheat, don't steal, don't kill, don't sleep around. According to these rules, he was already acting like Jesus. He dreamed of what he would say in two weeks, when he stood in front of that class—in front of Tina Lockhart and Camille and that dweeb Mitch and all those other sappy Christians. Maybe he'd begin his speech with, "If being a Christian means doing what Jesus would do, then I'm a Christian. And by the way, I'm also an *atheist*!" He imagined the looks on their faces, and laughed.

Of course, to back up his claims he'd have to read the fables. He knew almost nothing about Jesus, except that he'd died on a cross. "A sacrifice," Mitch had once told him after his teammate had returned from some Christian summer camp and tried to convert everyone on the team. There was no way Matt was going to ask Mitch for help now—especially since Mitch hadn't even volunteered for the experiment. No, Matt would learn about Jesus straight from the book. The Bible.

After work, Matt walked around the corner to Read It Again, Sam, a used-book store. A big reader, Matt had gone into that store often enough. But he had never been to the religion section. On the bottom shelf he found a bunch of books titled *Holy Bible*. He was surprised there was such a variety— several different sizes, covers, and conditions. He grabbed the most battered copy—a large paperback, its cover torn and the pages dog-eared. Two bucks.

As he walked to the register, he looked around to make sure no one he knew was there to see him. All clear. The clerk recognized him, but didn't say anything about his purchase.

"Wanna bag?"

Matt shook his head, stuffed the book into his backpack, and walked out of the store feeling like he had just bought a dirty magazine.

When he got home, Matt went straight to his room, sat at his desk, and pulled out the tattered

book. He flipped through it, hoping to find Jesus'
name somewhere on the pages, but came up with
nothing. Then he turned back to the table of contents. There were dozens and dozens of chapters
with bizarre names like *Deuteronomy, Ezra,
Lamentations, Obadiah, Thessalonians*—but no
Jesus. *What kind of religious book doesn't even
mention the hero in the contents!* Matt wondered.

He was just about to give up and move on to
something productive, like checking his email,
when his eye caught his own name. "The Gospel
According to *Matthew*." He found "Jesus" in the
first line: "A record of the genealogy of Jesus Christ
the son of David, the son of Abraham."

5

Getting Serious

Tina followed Danny's truck back to his house in her own car. Actually, it was her mom's minivan. She was hoping to get her own car for graduation, but until then, she made do with borrowing her mom's, or letting Danny chauffeur her in his four-by-four.

"Go see what's on," Danny said as they entered the empty house. "I'll grab us something to eat."

"Forget food. I'm not hungry," she whined, trying to guide him back to the den with her.

"Of course not! You ate all the preschoolers' cookies. And by the way, thanks for saving some for me."

"I had two, maybe three cookies!"

"Well, you taste like you had more," he joked. He gave her a quick kiss, this shook his head.

He slipped into the kitchen, sending Tina to the den alone. The room was more like a home theater, with a giant TV, speakers in every corner, and a big leather couch in the middle. Tina hunted among the arsenal of remotes lined up on the coffee table, trying to find the one that spoke to the TV. She accidentally turned on the CD player, then the VCR, and was still fumbling for the TV's on button when Danny came in with a bag of chips.

"You *still* haven't figured out how to run this stuff?"

"How can I? There's, like, a million of these little things, and they all look the same!"

"My mom can't figure it out either. That's why she makes my dad lay them out alphabetically!" Danny rearranged the remotes on the table. "Stereo. TV. VCR. Get it?"

As they sank onto the couch together, Tina kicked the remotes into a pile. "No, I don't get it. Explain it to me again!"

"What a troublemaker," he laughed, smacking her leg. "Better watch out, or I'll tell my dad." He grabbed the TV remote and began flipping through the channels.

"Go ahead," Tina taunted, tickling him. "He likes *me* more than *you*."

"You got *that* right! You've got him wrapped around your little finger. But he doesn't like you as much as *I* like you." Danny pulled her closer, then filled his mouth with a great handful of potato chips.

"Ooh, how romantic!" Tina purred, wiping the crumbs from his face.

"So tell me about this experiment thing you were all talking about in the kitchen. Apparently, I missed out on more than cookies."

Tina didn't feel like talking about it, so she gave him a short summary, hoping that would be the end of it. Usually, she was delighted by his ability to listen. Danny showed lots of interest in whatever she said, and he knew how to ask good questions that proved he was paying attention. She figured that was one of the reasons they had been together so long—their six-month anniversary was next week. With other guys she had dated, she had quickly grown tired of listening to their one-sided conversations.

Danny was different. He was persistent in everything—he knew how to get what he wanted. When he locked onto a topic, he stayed there till there was nothing left to talk about. His appearance helped. Tall, broad-shouldered, with a square jaw, keen eyes, and subtle, closed-mouth smile, when he asked questions, he got answers—usually because people wanted to give them, but sometimes because they couldn't help themselves. It was no wonder he wanted to be a lawyer. He'd be good at it.

But tonight Danny's questions were starting to bug her. He kept asking about the experiment, making too big a deal out of it—just as Camille and Mitch and Amanda had done. After dropping several hints and trying to steer the conversation elsewhere—including asking him about his next big plans for tricking out his truck, which always got him talking—she took a direct approach. "I'm sick of talking about this stupid experiment! Can we just watch TV?"

Danny apologized, turned down the lights, and curled up with Tina on the couch.

* * *

The two said goodnight before Danny's parents came home, and Tina drove the few miles back to her house. She was troubled by what had just happened with Danny, and what that meant in light of the experiment. The drive was too short for answers. When she pulled into the driveway, she shut off the engine and sat in the darkness to sort it all out.

She had worked hard to convince everyone that the experiment was no big deal, but now she was starting to doubt her own conclusion. In most ways, she was what her youth minister described as a true, committed Christian. She got along with her folks. She was active in the church. She read her Bible often and tried to remember to pray for her friends. And best of all, she was never afraid to stand up for her faith at school—to challenge teachers, witness to others. She even helped found the Christian club on campus. All things considered, she figured she was already doing what Jesus would do.

Except for one thing. Danny.

It's not like we're sleeping together, she rationalized, but still, sometime in the last month they had crossed a line. At first she didn't really know it as a line. It wasn't something they had talked about, made a rule about. But afterward, she felt uncomfortable and self-conscious and, well, *guilty*. She didn't know she had gone far enough until it felt like *too* far.

She had no idea of what Danny thought. They didn't talk about it. They could talk about anything, but why not this? She kept wishing he would bring it up, but he never did. She had considered making the first move, but then he might want to talk *too much* about it, cross-examining her like he did whenever they talked about something unpleasant.

Things were easier to deal with in her last relationship. When Kevin started pressuring her to be more physical, she got mad and said no. He got ticked and they broke up. Actually, he broke up with her. But in the end, it was no great loss, and soon she was dating Danny—a much finer catch. Maybe too good. The last thing she wanted was to lose him. What if she said no? Would he respect that? Or would he find someone else?

Then came the *big* question: What would Jesus do? How could she possibly know the answer? She could think of plenty of stories telling what Jesus did in all sorts of situations. But not *this* situation. He never married, never had a dating relationship. *If I did what Jesus did, I'd never have another date!* And if *everyone* did what Jesus did with the opposite sex, no one would be alive to even ask the question! No marriage, no sex, no children.

But that was silly. *The question isn't What did Jesus do?—it's What would he do if he were in my shoes?* That put it all in a different light. She didn't like what she saw. It was a picture of her talking to Danny about their physical relationship . . . and Danny didn't look happy.

This experiment might turn out to be a big deal after all.

6

Hard Not to Like

It took Matt less than two hours to read the story that had his name on it. He could have finished it in less time, but he took it slow, using a yellow high-lighting pen to mark the paragraphs that he thought would be useful in preparing his report. By the time he got to the end, he was pretty confused.

On the one hand, the Jesus in the fable matched Matt's expectations: He made big moral speeches, pulled off all sorts of far-fetched miracles, and talked about God a lot. In short, it was a bunch of stuff writ-ten to convince suckers that *this* religion was better than the others. Just like all the other religious myths they had studied in World Religions class.

On the other hand, this same Jesus did stuff that was totally unexpected. He hung out with the work-ing class, poor people, young people, and even some real losers. He took care of people who were sick—and even touched a guy with leprosy. He said that people who exploited children would be bet-ter off dead! He ran through the religious flea mar-ket, flipping over tables! He broke the rules, and when the conceited religious leaders confronted him about his behavior, he told them they were full of crap! Or something like that.

This Jesus character questioned authority, practiced civil disobedience, acted as an advocate for the poor and oppressed—he was *not* what you expected in a religious hero. Jesus was a rebel, an Antee. In many ways, Jesus was like Matt.

That's what troubled him the most. Despite Matt's contempt for Christianity, there was too much about this Jesus guy that he actually liked. Sure, his story had some *major* flaws—all his talk about "the Father" got old fast, and that ridiculous "resurrection" episode was a joke. But nobody's perfect—not even in a myth.

The good thing was, this might make Matt's experiment easier. He already agreed with much of what the Jesus character said and did. So acting like Jesus just meant acting like himself ... on a good day, anyway. And if he messed up every once in a while, well, Jesus wasn't perfect either.

Before setting down the book, he paged back through the Matthew section. There were yellow marks on nearly every page, highlighting the stuff both Matthews agreed was good enough to study again.

7

Breakfast with Jesus

"I must be dreaming!"

Tina looked up from the eggs she was scrambling to see her mom, still in her robe, pretending to wipe sleep from her eyes.

"What has gotten into *you* so early on a Saturday morning?"

"I thought I'd make everyone breakfast."

"How sweet of you!" her mom exclaimed, then planted a kiss on her cheek for emphasis. "And it looks like you're almost done—I'd better rally the troops." She left the kitchen to check on Tina's stepdad, Mike, and her two stepbrothers, who were staying with them for the weekend.

Tina smirked as she set the table. She had known that her mom would be surprised to find her making breakfast for everyone. She would be even more surprised if she knew *why* Tina was making breakfast.

The truth was, Tina was surprised herself. She certainly hadn't planned on anything like this when she fell asleep last night. But she had awakened early, which was odd, considering how tired she had been last night and how much she liked to sleep in on Saturday mornings. When she opened her eyes, she caught sight of her Bible on the night stand, where it had sat unopened since last weekend. It reminded her of the experiment, and her thoughts about Danny, and that troubling question, "What would Jesus do?"

Still in bed, she opened her Bible to the bookmark and began reading in John's gospel, chapter 13. The fifth verse caught her attention: "After that, he poured water into a basin and began to wash his disciples' feet, drying them with the towel that was wrapped around him."

Tina had read that verse many times before and was sure she had heard sermons and youth talks about it, although she couldn't remember what had been said. But this time it struck her as strange that Jesus would wrap a towel around his waist, get down on the floor, and wash people's dirty feet.

When she witnessed to people, she often told them that Jesus was a "servant." But what did that mean, really? He wasn't acting like those cashiers at the fast food places, all dressed alike in their crisp uniforms, and all using that canned, insincere greeting, "How may I serve you today?" Jesus didn't stand around waiting to take orders. He just got down on his knees and did the dirty work.

She closed her Bible and prayed: *Help me to do what you would do. Help me to be a servant.* And then she thought of making breakfast for the family. It wasn't the same as washing feet—but then again, Jesus had never smelled her step-brothers' socks.

When the "troops" arrived, they were pleasantly shocked to see Tina's feast waiting for them.

"What'd you do all this for, *Teenie*?" Michael jested. "Put another dent in the car?"

Tina just smiled and hit him on the head with the hot pad. Michael had come up with that nickname on his thirteenth birthday last summer when he figured out that at 5' 4", he towered above her by a full inch. But whenever his ten-year-old brother Brad tried calling her Teenie, she'd pick him up and say, "What was that, Brad-*lee*?" For younger brothers, they were pretty good—especially when you compared them to Amanda's little brother, who was a brat. Then again, Amanda had to contend with her brother every day; Tina's were around just every other weekend.

Breakfast table conversation was dominated by Michael's and Brad's soccer exploits, which the two recounted in numbing detail. Afterward, the boys went shopping with their dad while Tina and her mom cleaned up.

They chatted as they worked—school stuff, the musical, Danny's college plans. Then, hesitantly, half-afraid that her mom would use it against her, Tina explained the experiment. From her mom's quiet "Aha," she figured that her mom now grasped her reason for preparing breakfast.

Even so, Tina enjoyed their talk. It was refreshingly casual and "normal"—like the conversations they used to have all the time but were rare now that Tina was driving and dating and pouring herself into church activities. Just last week, her mom had joked, "Tina, you're never home anymore. Don't you love us?"

But now, as they talked, laughed, washed, and dried, she wondered if her mom had been only half-joking. She *was* gone a lot. Of course, she did spend most of her free time in youth group activities— Bible studies, retreats, service projects, and lately, the musical. These were all *good* things, *Christian* things, opportunities to serve others. But still, they took her away from serving her family.

What would Jesus do?

There was that question again.

8

Confession

Tina spent the rest of the morning practicing her lines. Today was their first dress rehearsal—and their last chance to get it all together before tomorrow night's performance. She had the singing parts down—words were easier to remember set to music. The spoken parts were still a bit rough, but by the time she left for rehearsal, she had them pretty tight.

Pulling into the church parking lot, she remembered what she had read that morning in her Bible. How could she serve her friends better that day? *Just be nicer* was all she could come up with.

Mitch was carrying a big box of props when Tina ran into him outside the senior-high room. "Hey, let me help you."

"Hi, Tina. Thanks!"

She grabbed one end, and the two muscled the box down the hall.

"So how you doing with that experiment?" Mitch grunted.

"Okay, I guess." She thought of telling him about serving breakfast for her family that morning, but figured it might sound like bragging. "But to be honest, I'm having a hard time remembering to ask the 'What would Jesus do?' question."

"Do what I do when I have to remember something."

"What's that?" asked Tina, trying to sound like she cared.

"Here, I'll show you." Mitch steered them to a table at the end of the hall and shoved the box onto it. He dug a pen from his pocket and grabbed her hand. "I write down the initials to remind me." He printed "WWJD?" on the heel of her palm. She was so startled by his boldness that she didn't even think to pull back her hand. "There. Whenever you look at your hand, you'll remember it!"

"Mitch! I can't believe you just wrote on my hand! Now I'll have this big ink blotch on me."

"Yeah, but think of it this way: Jesus had big nail holes in *his* hands."

"Great! Next time I see you with a hammer, I'll know to run."

They picked up the box and headed outside, across the courtyard toward the auditorium. Tina looked down and saw the blue initials staring up at her where her hand bulged around the box corner. "You know, Mitch, I wanted to apologize for how I treated you last night."

Mitch looked confused. "Why? What'd you do?"

"I was mad at you for telling everyone about what happened in Veras's class."

"You were? It didn't seem like it. Hey, I'm sorry for blabbing it all. I didn't even think about it."

"Don't apologize, Mitch! You didn't do anything wrong. I'm the one who should be apologizing."

"There's nothing to apologize about."

"Yes there is. I got mad at you for a stupid reason. And not just last night. The thing is, well ... I don't always treat you very well." Mitch looked embarrassed—probably because he had never heard her speak that way to him. She continued. "Like at school."

"You treat me just fine at school."

"No, I don't. You *know* I don't."

Mitch shifted his end of the box, looking down like he was deciding whether to say something. "Well, sometimes, when we pass in the hall, and you're with your friends ... but I figure you're busy and talking about something important and that's why you don't say hi. Which is totally understandable and I'm sure I walk past you sometimes and I'm in my own world and don't see you either. And anyway, if I were a senior, I'm sure I wouldn't say hi to every geeky sophomore who walked past me, just because I knew them from church."

In his own blundering way, he was trying to make her feel better, but his awkward grace for her own arrogance made it sting all the more. She jumped in before he said anything more. "I doubt that. You're too nice a guy. I guess I get caught up in *my* own little world and forget to treat people

the way they deserve. I know I've been doing that
with you, and—well—I'm just *sorry*."

They had reached the door to the auditorium,
which was good because Tina didn't know what
else to say. Mitch just smiled, nodded his head, and
propped up the box on his knee to open the door.
As they carried the box to the stage, Tina glanced
down at her hand again and said, "Hey, I guess your
little reminder trick works."

"Told ya."

"C'mon, Mitchell!" It was Amanda, who had
walked in just as they were setting down the box.
"Show some muscle! You shouldn't need Tina's
help to carry that little box!"

"Shut up, Amanda," Tina said, only half-joking.
"This thing is heavy!" After her talk with Mitch,
Amanda's remark seemed especially harsh—and a
bit too close to home, as she remembered saying even
meaner things to him in the past.

As Mitch walked away, Amanda caught sight
of the blue letters on Tina's hand. "What's that?"

"Nothing. Just a little reminder Mitch put there."

"What's it stand for?"

"'What would Jesus do?' It's to help me
remember the experiment."

"How *cute*! But you better not let Danny see it.
He won't be happy if he finds out that some other
guy has been touching his woman." Amanda said
the last part with a deep, Danny-like voice.

"So what?" Tina said, a bit too seriously.

"Lighten *up*, girlfriend—I'm only kidding!" Amanda grabbed her friend's arm and led her backstage to get into costume.

9

Service

"That was great!" Tina said. "You have such a pretty voice."

Maria, who had just finished her solo, almost jumped when she heard the compliment. "Thank you, Tina! Yours too!"

Tina accepted the returned compliment with a smile, but thought, *Why is everyone acting so surprised?* At intermission, when Tina had stopped to help some of the freshman girls with their costumes, they had reacted the same way. Jacob too. All she had said to him was, "Sorry I messed you up last night in the final scene—thanks for covering for me." It was true—she had forgotten her line—but why had he acted so surprised to hear her admit it?

Am I really that cliquish, that cold, when I'm not trying to be nice? It seemed simple to Tina— she was just looking out for others, trying to offer help and encouragement. But obviously, it wasn't what people expected from her.

After the final scene, Amanda whispered, "What's got into you?"

"I don't know what you mean," Tina lied, knowing exactly what her friend meant.

"You've been avoiding us all night," Amanda shot back. "We're starting to wonder."

"Who's *we?*"

"Your *friends*, that's who."

It was true—she *had* been avoiding Danny, Amanda, and a few of the other leading seniors who clung together at every church event. But she knew that if she retreated to the safety of her regular friends, she'd chicken out on the "be nice to the others" plan.

When the rehearsal ended, Tina changed out of her costume and walked backstage to find Amanda. A small group of kids was huddled in her path, talking quietly. But as Tina approached, they stopped talking.

"Naughty, naughty," Tina said, feigning a stern look and shaking her finger. "You know what the Bible says about gossiping." Then she added in a whisper, "So who are we gossiping about?"

Silence. Everyone looked at each other, or at the ground—anywhere but at her. Tina panicked. Her mind raced through the options: *Has someone been spreading lies about me? Do they know something about Danny and me? Did Amanda say something to them?* She spoke as calmly as possible. "I see. So what are you saying about me?"

More silence. Finally, Maria spoke up. "Sorry, Tina. We were just saying that you're acting . . . *different*."

One of the freshman girls followed up. "It's, like, you're such a great person and everything— but tonight you just seemed *especially* nice."

Jacob jumped in. "Mitch mentioned something about an experiment in school—"

"Me and my big mouth again," confessed Mitch, as Tina gave him a look.

"And we were wondering," Jacob continued, "if that was the reason why you're being so nice to everyone."

"Is that it?" asked Maria. "Tell us about it."

Tina was embarrassed and felt a little like she was in the witness stand—or at least, like she was back on stage. But she felt relieved, too. They *could* have been talking about something far worse. She looked down, trying to think of what to say, and spotted the "WWJD?" on her hand.

She started to tell them what had happened in class yesterday, but by the way they were nodding their heads, she figured Mitch had already explained that part. So she skipped to what she had read in her Bible that morning. At that point, Amanda joined the circle, listening curiously as Tina spoke to this group of people whom the two had always smiled at, been polite to, but otherwise ignored.

"It just kind of hit me," Tina continued, "that part about Jesus being a servant. Maybe 'doing what Jesus would do' means serving each other better."

Someone out on stage shouted, "Refreshments!" Apparently Jim had figured out that good work deserved a reward, so he was serving legitimate snacks back in the kitchen.

The group broke up, but Mitch, Jacob, and Maria looked like they wanted to talk some more.

"Are you coming?" asked Amanda impatiently.

"Go ahead—I'll be there in a minute. Save something for me!"

Amanda turned and left, looking displeased.

"We were wondering if we could join your experiment," said Maria, whose boldness reminded her of Danny's, except that she was less intimidating.

"How can you? You're not even in the class. And Mitch—you had your chance yesterday."

"We don't care about the class," said Maria. "We just think it's a good idea."

"And if more of us are doing it," added Jacob, "maybe we can support each other—help remind each other."

"Pray for each other," Mitch said, finishing the thought. "What do you think?"

Tina didn't know what to say. She had been thinking of it as *her* experiment, *her* opportunity to witness to people at school. And besides, these weren't exactly the people she would pick to join her if she had that choice.

Then again, it might be nice to have some support. After what Mitch said about that Matt Chen kid, she knew she wouldn't be getting any help from *him.* "Well, I guess. Sure, if you want to do it. I suppose anyone can do it if they want."

The three looked excited to hear her approval. Mitch made a corny ceremony out of it. He grabbed her hand and raised it between them. "Okay, everybody put your hand on Tina's. We promise, before every decision in the next two weeks, to ask the question, 'What would Jesus do?'—and then do it, *no matter what.* Say amen."

Everyone said amen, including Tina, who was thinking about Mitch's sneaky little addendum to the promise—"*no matter what.*"

Maria spoke next. "Shouldn't we pray or something?"

Jacob closed the ceremony in a short prayer.

When Tina left them to go find Amanda, Mitch had his pen out again. He was writing on everyone's hand.

10

The Picture

The house was empty when Tina got home. The note on the kitchen counter said they'd all gone to the amusement park. On weekends when Mike had the boys, they always did big fun things together. Tina went out to check the mail, hoping for an acceptance letter from one the colleges she had applied to. No such luck—just junk mail, a few bills addressed to Michael S. Carson, a magazine addressed to Joanne Carson.

And a letter addressed to *Martina Lockhart.*

Her stomach turned when she saw the name. No one called her Martina anymore. Not her mom, not her teachers, and certainly not her friends. The only one who still used *Martina* was her father.

She heard from him just once a year, when he sent her a birthday card, usually with a $50 check inside. Her birthday was three months away. Tina dropped the rest of the mail onto the kitchen counter and went to her room. She placed the unopened letter on her desk, then turned on her computer to check for email. There was a message from Amanda, just saying hi, and a nice note from Danny, telling her he was looking forward to their anniversary date next Friday. She started to type a

reply, but couldn't stop thinking about the letter.
She reached over and opened it.

It was a card with a photo attached to it. There
was her dad—with less hair than she remembered.
He was holding a little blonde-haired girl. Sitting next
to him was the "new" Mrs. Lockhart—the woman
he had left her mom for—holding up a red-faced
newborn baby. Beneath the photo was a caption:

"THE LOCKHART FAMILY

proudly welcomes its newest member

LINDA MARIE—"

Tina's eyes welled up till she couldn't read the
rest. She threw the card back onto the desk and sank
onto her bed.

And sobbed. She hadn't seen her dad since her
junior high graduation day. And now, there he was,
all smiles and pride, with his new daughter. "The
Lockhart *family*. What a lie!" she screamed to no
one. *"I'm* a Lockhart—the *first* Lockhart daughter,
and I'm not even in the family picture!"

Something floated through her mind: the summer before her eighth grade year, coming home
from church camp on that rainy afternoon, her
mother picking her up in their battered old car, driving her to a park rather than to their home. She
remembered sitting in the car, the engine running,
the slow beat of the wipers that couldn't keep up
with the rain that blurred the windshield, the plink-
ing of drops on the roof, the sound of her mom

telling her that her dad had moved out. Then nothing but the sound of them crying together.

When they got home, the apartment looked the same as when she'd left it a week earlier. Nothing was missing, nothing out of place. But that night, when she asked if she could sleep in her mom's bed, she saw the gap in the closet where her dad's clothes had once hung.

He had left a letter on her bed. It said he was sorry, that he loved her, that she was his little princess, but he had to go away, and would come and see her soon. It was weeks before she could sleep in her own bed again. Nearly a year before she heard from him.

She recalled almost nothing from her eighth grade year, except that they moved to a smaller apartment, and that her mom spent a lot of time at a lawyer's office and was angry a lot. What classes she had that year, what she and her friends did together—that was all a blur, like the rain on the windshield.

Until graduation day.

He showed up unannounced, uninvited. After the ceremony, as she and her friends stood and posed for pictures in front of their proud, camera-happy parents, he walked up out of nowhere, gave her a hug, a kiss, and a present. Then he vanished into the crowd.

It all happened so fast she didn't know what to feel, until she saw her mom with tears in her eyes, and then she cried too. In front of all her friends. The present was a pink dress that might have fit her in elementary school. She never saw him again.

After the divorce went through, her mom tried to get child support, but he sent little, then less, then nothing at all. Then her mom married Mike, who was rich compared to her dad, and decided that there was no point in wasting any more time and money trying to squeeze support out of her "deadbeat father"—better to get him out of their life. They moved into a big new house, her mom got a new car, and Tina got all new clothes, a stereo, a phone, and her own computer.

Over the nearly four years since she last saw him, Tina had nearly managed to block her father's existence out of her mind. Once a year, when she got a birthday card, he forced himself back in. But so much had happened in the last few years—the memories of her and her mom's new life with Mike were filling her head, squeezing out the painful memories of her old life with her old dad. With each passing year, her dad became less and less real to her, less like a *person* and more like a character in a sad story she once heard. It was easier to think of him as a distant something, rather than an important *someone*. It made it easier to hate him.

Tina's sobs subsided. Her stomach muscles felt like they'd just completed fifty sit-ups. The acute pain in her heart was passing, pushed out by a duller, more comfortable anger. As she swept the hair from her face, she saw the blue ink on her hand, now smudged from her tears.

11

Truth

Matt slept in on Saturday morning, then woke in a panic as he remembered that he had promised to show up for work early that day. He took a quick shower, barely beating his little brother to the bathroom, then shoved down a bowl of cereal, grabbed his coat and backpack, and made it out the door without running into his dad.

But halfway down the block, he spotted him, heading back from a morning run. His dad ran across the street to speak to him.

"Where are you headed?" He was out of breath.

"To work."

"Isn't it too early?"

"We're having a sale. I have to go in early."

"How'd you do on that geometry quiz yesterday?"

"Got a B," Matt lied, knowing his math-obsessed, engineer father would come unglued if he told him what he really got.

"Okay then, now you start working toward an A."

That was just like his dad—never satisfied, always wanting more. "I gotta go, I'm running late." Matt started walking away, but backwards, in case his dad had more to say—which he always did.

"What time will you be home?"

"I dunno. Whenever."

"Make it before ten."

"Okay, but I gotta go." Matt turned around and jogged down the street, but slowed to a walk as soon as he turned the corner, safely out of sight. He wasn't *that* late.

Usually, when he lied to his dad, he didn't give it a second thought. But this time, it bothered him. It wasn't guilt, really—just something uncomfortable. Then he remembered the assignment: Ask *What would Jesus do?*—and then do it.

Would that Jesus character have lied? *Maybe,* he rationalized, *if he thought that the truth would hurt the other person.* Jesus seemed to care more about others than he cared about himself, and he would have considered their feelings first. And Matt knew that his dad, if he had heard that Matt got a D on the quiz, would have gotten mad and maybe stayed upset all morning. *Why wreck his morning? He's better off not knowing.*

But somehow, that theory didn't really fit with the Jesus Matt had read about last night. When people didn't tell the truth, Jesus called them liars, or something like that. Would Jesus make a big deal about the truth, then lie himself? That didn't make sense. He wasn't that kind of guy.

Besides, lying would have seemed disrespect-ful. When someone asked Jesus a question, he cared enough about the person to tell the truth—even if that person was a loser. What Matt had done with his dad that morning had been disrespectful. His dad deserved the truth.

Really, telling the truth made sense. Everybody lied. Politicians lied—telling you one thing and then doing another. Some so-called charities, claiming they were using your donation to help the homeless, kept the money for themselves. And Christians lied when they said they loved everyone, then ended up hating you just because you didn't believe the same things they did. Lying was just acting like everyone else. Jesus was a rebel. He *didn't* act like everyone else. If everyone lied, Jesus would be the one guy who would tell the truth.

By the time he reached the store, Matt had made a resolution: *No more lying . . . at least for the next two weeks. And try to treat people with respect.*

* * *

"C'mon, Matthew dear," Laura whispered, as she and her friend Cindy stood at the checkout counter. "Give us that sweet discount."

It was no big deal, really. As an employee, Matt got a great discount on CDs, and his friends knew they could count on him to use it for their own purchases.

"I'm sorry, I just can't this time."

"Why not?" asked Cindy, looking peeved. She and her look-alike friend each had a CD.

"I just can't. They're already discounted—just buy them yourself. You have money!"

The two friends looked at each other, huffed, and walked out of the store, not even turning to acknowledge his "I'm sorry."

Matt re-shelved the CDs, angry at himself for not giving in, confused by this latest test. None of his friends, coworkers, and customers knew about the World Religions assignment or the resolution he made on his way to work that morning. But it was as if they did. All day Saturday, and again on Sunday, they acted like they were conspiring to trip him up. He tried to be nicer to people, to treat them with respect, to keep from lying, but he was getting hit from all sides.

He couldn't give Laura and Cindy his discount because it meant lying to Kathy, the manager. That hadn't been a problem before. *Everybody did it*, he used to reason. But Jesus wouldn't, so now he was stuck saying no to people who had learned to count on his lies.

A similar thing happened on Sunday, except this time it was Kathy herself asking him to lie. "It's your boyfriend," he said, after putting the caller on hold.

"Tell him I'm at lunch."

As he picked up the phone again, the question hit him: *Is that a lie?* He hesitated, glancing between Kathy and the phone. Her look said,

What's your problem? He turned his back to her and spoke softly into the phone.

When he hung up Kathy was right in his face. "I'm not *available?* I told you to say I was *at lunch!*"

"Sorry."

"Don't say you're sorry. Just do as I say. Now he's wondering what's up because you made it sound like I was here, but I didn't want to speak to him."

Which is true enough, Matt felt like saying.

At least a dozen such challenges confronted Matt throughout the weekend. Opportunities to lie, cheat on his hours, fudge the truth, to tell off rude customers. Truth and respect were turning out to be full-time jobs. By Sunday night, Matt was convinced that Jesus was more of a rebel than he had thought. And acting like Jesus was tougher than it looked.

12

Unofficial

Tina bowed her head for Pastor Jim's closing prayer. As always, Jim worked the entire Sunday school lesson's outline into his prayer—one last chance to make his message stick. Tina was still praying silently about personal things when she heard him end his prayer and say to the group: "One more thing. I've heard some talk about an 'experiment.' If you know what I'm talking about, please stay for another minute. The rest of you—we'll see you tonight for the big show!"

The room cleared out quickly. Tina sat in her chair, wondering how many of the other experimenters would stay behind. Mitch got to Jim first—no surprise, since he always sat in the front row. Jacob said goodbye to some friends, then made his way to the front. Maria spotted Tina and waved her forward; she was with that new freshman girl—Shelly or Sherrie or something.

"Maria, I ran into your mom today after the service," said Jim, when the five had sat down in the front. "She was very excited about this *experiment* we were conducting in the youth group. So before I run into her again, maybe you folks can tell me about this experiment that *we* are doing."

"I'm sorry," Maria replied, "I didn't tell her it was an official youth group thing—I just said it was something that some of us in the youth group were doing. She must have got it mixed up."

"That's fine—I'm not upset." said Jim, looking just a little upset. "But I *would* like to know what it is."

"It's a good thing, really! But it wasn't my idea. It was Tina's."

Oh great, Tina thought. *Now it's all on my shoulders.*

Jim turned to her, anxious for an answer.

"It all started in my World Religions class at school on Friday . . ."

"That's great!" Jim exclaimed, when she had finished her story. He looked impressed—especially when he heard that his Bible study lesson had given her the original idea. "But what about the rest of you? You're not all in Tina's class."

Mitch told how he had chickened out that day in Ms. Veras's class—and why, after seeing how Tina was acting last night at rehearsal, he and the others had asked if they could join her anyway. "We made a promise, then wrote down these initials on our hands to remind us." He held up his hand to show Jim. " 'What would Jesus do?' Get it?"

"I get it," Jim said. "But—" He hesitated. "Not all of you were there last night."

Tina looked at the others. The only one not in the musical was Shawna or Sheila or whatever her name was. Apparently, she wasn't the only one who had forgotten the new girl's name.

Maria saved him. "Shannon wasn't there, but I called her last night when I got home, and she said she wanted to join." The new girl nodded her head, but said nothing.

"Well, I've got to tell you," Jim continued, "I'm very impressed with this idea. And Tina, I'm thrilled to know you actually heard something I said at Bible study!" She smiled, but didn't interrupt. "As you guys were telling me about it just now, I was thinking how great it would be to make this an official youth group program."

Mitch gave an amen.

"But now I'm not so sure. Tina, whatever reason you had for making that promise in class on Friday, I've got to believe that the Holy Spirit was at work in there somewhere. The rest of you are proof to that. You saw something different in Tina last night, and that prompted you to want that thing too. That's exactly how the Holy Spirit works. One to one, person to person, he infects the people around us by changing who we are, what we say, how we act. That's obviously what has been happening with you guys. So let's keep it that way. Let's see how this fire spreads. I'll pray for you, I'll support you, I'll help you in any way you want. But this is *your* experiment—or the Holy Spirit's, really—and I trust that he's going to do bigger things with it than I could do by standing up here and preaching about it. What do you think?"

Jacob spoke for the first time. "I think you're right. No offense, but maybe if you made it into a project, some kids would treat it like something they *have* to do. This way, it'll be something they *want* to do—like we did last night. And if it dies—like that fund-raising idea we had earlier in the year—"

"Hey!" The fund-raiser flop was partly Mitch's idea.

"No offense, Mitch. But what I'm saying is, if nothing happens from this experiment thing, it'll be because *we* dropped the ball, not because Jim had a bad day and didn't preach it right."

"Hey!" grunted Jim, mimicking Mitch and smiling at him too. "Tina, you started this whole thing—are you okay about keeping it 'unofficial'?"

"Sure, but that doesn't mean I'm in charge of it." *I'm busy enough just trying to live it myself*, she added, but not out loud.

"Of course not," Mitch said. "We'll let Jesus be in charge."

Jim stood. "Speaking of Jesus, do you mind if I ask him to guide you in your experiment?"

After Jim's prayer, as Tina walked out of the senior high room, Maria caught up with her. "Can I give you something?"

Tina was taken aback. Maria hardly knew her well enough to be giving her things. "I guess. What is it?"

Maria pulled a thin red ribbon from her pocket. It had "WWJD?" printed on it in simple bold letters. "I made it last night. The ink is waterproof. I figured you wouldn't want to be walking around school with stuff written on your hand!" She grabbed Tina's hand and tied the ribbon around her wrist.

"Thank you! That's sweet!" Tina managed to sound more pleased than she was. What would her friends say if she actually wore it to school?

"I made one for myself. Would you tie it for me?"

Tina tied the ribbon around Maria's wrist, and as she did, the thought occurred to her: *Why was my first thought about my own appearance, rather than feeling grateful for this kindness from a girl I hardly know?*

13

Before the Show

"Hey girlfriend! Wow—your hair looks great!" said Amanda, sitting in front of the mirror in the dressing room when Tina arrived to get ready for the musical.

"It better! It only took me all afternoon." Tina took off her coat and tossed it on a chair.

Amanda spun around and grabbed her friend's wrist. "What's this?"

"Maria gave it to me," said Tina, wishing Amanda hadn't spotted it. "It's to remind me of the experiment. No big deal."

"Oh." Amanda spun back in her chair to fix her makeup. "So, what did Jim have to say after Sunday school?"

Amanda was obviously trying to act nonchalant, but Tina knew her friend too well to buy the act. "Nothing. He just wanted to know what the experiment was about, so we explained it to him."

"*We*? I thought you and that Antee kid were the only ones who volunteered?" Amanda was staring at her through eyelash brush and mirror.

"After you left last night, Mitch, Maria, and Jacob asked if they could do it too. I know, I know—they're not part of the classroom experiment. But they thought it was a good idea and wanted to join it."

"Great! Next thing I know, you'll be asking me to join your little club."

"'Manda, it's not a *club*, and I didn't ask them to join. They asked *me*. If they want to do it too, it's their business. It has nothing to do with me."

"So you *don't* want me to join."

"That's not it at all! You can do it if you want, or not do it—I'm fine either way." Tina sat down and touched Amanda's arm. "*Please* stopping asking me about it."

Amanda finally let up. "I'm sorry. I'm just a little nervous about tonight. How 'bout you? You seem a little stressed."

That was an understatement. As Tina turned and looked into the mirror, her hair was right, but the face it framed revealed the turmoil inside—a snarled mess of performance jitters, guilt, doubt, anxiety, and questions about the musical, the experiment, Danny, her father. The reflection blurred.

"What is it? Did something happen with Danny?" Amanda's pettiness was gone.

"No—well, yes, but that's not really it. I got a card from my father yesterday."

Now Amanda's eyes welled up too. Among all Tina's friends, Amanda was the only one she had told about her father. Tina felt her friend's hand on her arm. "But your birthday isn't for months. Why'd he write you now? What did he say?"

"If I start telling you now, I won't be able to stop crying. But I need to talk about it. Can we wait till after the show?"

"Of course. You know I'm here for you." Amanda held Tina's hand. "We'll have a really great show, and make people stand up and cheer for more! And then afterward, we can talk all about it and have a good cry!"

"You're the best," Tina whispered, squeezing her hand.

"No, *you're* the best!"

After Amanda left the dressing room, Tina slid into her costume, fixed her makeup, and headed backstage.

Maria found her in the hall. "Tina, I'm really, really nervous! Can you please pray with me?"

"Right here?" She felt a little embarrassed standing in the middle of the hall, with cast and crew frantically running and shouting past them.

"Sure. I'll start." Maria bowed her head and began. But instead of praying for the whole cast, or the audience, or herself, she prayed for Tina. That touched Tina more than the prayer itself.

When Maria paused, Tina returned the gesture, praying only for the girl next to her, forgetting for a moment all the other concerns crowding her heart. When they finished praying, Maria pulled back the cuff of her costume to show Tina the "WWJD?" ribbon on her wrist. Tina started to pull back her own cuff but Maria stopped her with a hearty hug. She was so startled she let out a laugh.

"What's so funny?" Maria asked as she let go.

"Nothing—it's just that—I don't know. All of a sudden, I felt my heart get lighter."

14

Showtime

The musical went off without a hitch. Tina remembered all her lines, stayed in key and on tempo in her singing parts, and even had time to notice how well everyone else did—and to praise them for it. After Maria finished her solo, she stepped backstage and held out her hand for a high five. Tina was so surprised she returned it. "You nailed it!" Tina said.

"Your prayer worked!" Maria replied.

When it was over, Tina looked out into the cheering crowd to spot her folks. They were standing, but so was everyone else, which made the ovation all the sweeter. Afterward, she and her friends stood for pictures and congratulations, then adjourned to the dressing rooms to change out of their costumes.

Jim threw them a strike party, with enough pizza, ice cream, and sodas to feed a cast twice their size. It was a good thing he ordered plenty of food—many kids who weren't in the cast showed up to help strike the stage, and of course Jim let them join the party. The night turned into so much fun—and such a relief—that Tina almost forgot her troubles.

She spent the first half of the party mixing with people she'd never before hung out with: Maria and her friends, Jacob and his, and even nerdy Mitch, who didn't seem to have his own group of friends, but made up for it by floating from one table to the next, telling the corniest jokes imaginable.

Eventually, she looked for her "regular" friends. As usual, they had claimed their own table in the corner, where they were polishing off two whole pizzas commandeered from the serving line. As she approached them, she heard Amanda complaining because Jim had let non-cast members into the party. Danny agreed. He had supervised the tear-down of the staging and backdrops, where he'd watched a dozen "volunteers" put in about ten minutes of easy work just so they could get in on the food. "We do most of the work," he groused, "and they get the reward."

Tina was suddenly reminded of Jesus' parable about a bunch of workers who put in different numbers of hours in the field, yet got paid the same at the end of the day. But she said nothing. In fact, since none of her friends had noticed her approaching, she turned and wandered away from the gripe session and found Mitch telling the stupidest joke she had ever heard. She laughed so hard she almost shot Diet Coke from her nose. She was one of those rare people who got full from drinking just half a can. Drinking two whole cans, not to mention the chocolate sundae, had her so hopped up on caffeine that even Mitch's jokes now seemed funny.

In the middle of her laugh, Tina happened to look at Amanda, scowling at her from across the room. The cheery effects of caffeine and fellowship evaporated from that one look. Tina remembered her worries and walked over to Amanda to share them.

Danny was telling everyone a story, so Tina leaned over and whispered in her ear. "Don't forget that talk you promised me."

"What do you need *me* for?" Amanda replied, loud enough for the others to hear. "It looks like you're doing just fine without me."

Danny stopped mid-sentence while everyone looked up at Tina. There was no point in whispering. "But I'd still like to talk."

"It's kind of late. Can it wait till tomorrow? We can talk after school." Amanda immediately turned around, looked at Danny and said, "So finish your story, *Daniel.*"

Tina turned and walked toward the door. Danny grabbed her shoulder halfway across the room. "What was *that* about?"

"We were going to talk, that's all. I guess she doesn't feel like it now."

"Is everything okay? You've been kind of quiet these last two days. I'm getting the feeling that you're avoiding me."

His little smile told her he was only half-serious. Even so, he was completely right. She *had* been avoiding him. Since Friday night, she had been haunted by the guilt of their increasingly physical relationship. The guilt had been there before as a quiet, occasional discomfort, simple to disregard. But now it was loud, nagging, persistent. She didn't have a solution yet—or at least, no solution that she thought she could live with. Nor did she want to make things worse by getting into that situation again. It was easier to distance herself from Danny till she figured things out.

"Things are okay. I've just had a lot on my mind with the performance. And I've been thinking about that experiment for Veras's class." That was about as far as she could go without triggering a cross-examination. But to be sure, she put on a smile and switched topics. "Hey, thanks for your email about our anniversary. Very sweet. I'm looking forward to Friday."

"Me too!"

She kissed him on the cheek. "I'm really tired right now. I think I'll go home. See you tomorrow?"

Her parents were already in bed when she got home, which was good because she was not in the mood to talk. The fun of the strike party had been wiped out by Amanda's cold look and colder shoulder. Now she was left with that emptiness that comes when something long anticipated is

finally over, and there's nothing left to look forward to.

That alone was bad enough. But the musical
had served her in another way. The production had
distracted her from the big questions about Danny
and from this latest emotional assault from her past.
Now the show was over, leaving her with nothing
but those disturbing thoughts. She crawled into bed
and silently cried herself to sleep.

15

Antee Matter

Matt was actually relieved when Monday morning finally arrived. His "no lying" resolution had made things tough for him at the record store. And his brief conversations with his dad were no fun either. At least at school he could be among his friends—people who appreciated him, respected him, liked him just the way he was.

At lunch he spotted Laura and Cindy, who had arrived first at their regular table. From the back it was almost impossible to tell who was who. They were the same height and body shape and always dressed alike. Last year Cindy had even dyed her dirty blonde hair to match Laura's natural black mane. When they were together—which was pretty much all the time—their friends dispensed with their individual names and just called them collectively *Lindy*.

Matt sneaked up behind them and set a bag on the table.

"What's this, Matthew?" one Lindy asked. The other opened the bag and pulled out the two CDs they had tried so hard to buy yesterday. "Thank you!"

Cindy dug into her purse. "How much do we owe you?"

"Don't worry about it. It's a gift." That was the truth. He had bought the CDs with money he'd been saving for music for himself. But he would wait another month for his own music. As long as he used his own money to buy CDs on his employee discount, the store didn't care what he did with them.

Lindy thanked him again, and gave him part of their lunch too. That was one thing about the Antees—they were generous with each other. That came in handy at lunch time, because Matt was often short on cash. Most of his paycheck went to pay back his dad, who had loaned him the money for his new computer. And most of what was left was spent at the store on albums and computer games, or around the corner on used books.

The table was starting to fill up. Sarah was secretly showing everyone her new kitten, which she had managed to keep hidden in her giant coat pocket all day. Sarah was always doing the unexpected—sometimes on a dare, but most of the time on her own. The day before Christmas break, someone had dared her to sing a Christmas carol in the lunch room. She had jumped on the table and belted out "Rudolph the Red-Nosed Reindeer" in front of the whole school. Matt and his friends had given her a standing ovation, but other students had shouted "Freak!" or thrown food. Last month, she had found a sick bird outside the school and insisted on nursing it the rest of the day. When Mr. Pinchot had heard the bird squawking in French class, he sent her to the office. She had walked home instead.

Vinny walked up, interrupting the kitten-ogling. "Hey—anyone feel like sneaking into that debate?"

Chad raised his head, interested. "Oh yeah, that's today. What are the Jesus Freaks arguing about this time?"

"Jesus Christ—Fact or Fiction," one Lindy answered, in a comically low and serious voice. That was what the fliers said, posted on bulletin boards all over school. The campus Christian club hosted a different debate every month.

"Not another bogus debate!" the other Lindy complained. "They always rig them. Only members from their stupid club are allowed to speak, and the 'correct' argument always wins!"

"What a surprise!" added Lindy number one.

Vinny squeezed into a seat between Sarah and Matt. Apparently, he had given up on the debate idea. "Yeah, but it was fun to heckle them that one time."

"A lot of good *that* did us!"

"Yeah, I enjoyed that 'freedom of religion' lecture in the vice-principal's office."

"Lieutenant Les conveniently forgot about freedom of *speech*."

Matt hadn't joined in the Antees' invasion of the Christian club debate last fall, which had ended with his friends' trip to the vice-principal's office.

But he had had uncomfortable dealings with "the lieutenant" at other times, and had a pretty good picture of what it must have looked like.

Cindy added, "Besides, those debates are just a trap to get us *pagans* to join their little Jesus cult."

"If they had their way, we'd all be like robots, dressed in preppy clothes, and acting like Jesus." As if on cue, the Lindys primped each other's hair.

Sarah looked up from her kitten. "Didn't Jesus wear a *robe*?" She didn't mean it to be funny, but laughed when everyone else did.

"They don't act like Jesus anyway," Matt offered. "Jesus was nothing like that."

The others looked at him curiously. It *was* a strange thing for him to say. "How would *you* know, Mr. Atheist?" asked Laura.

Matt dismissed the question by explaining what he meant. "Christians all huddle together in their own little group, looking down on weird people like us, scared that we'll corrupt them. Jesus hung out with weird people. He couldn't stand being with people who acted all religious."

"Yeah, right." Vinny wasn't buying it.

"No lie," Matt shot back, a little too enthusiastically. "He hung out with lepers and homeless people and foreigners and people who weren't religious. And a lot of the stuff that he said for Christians to do—Christians don't even do. They judge people, and Jesus said don't judge. They fight back, and Jesus said that when someone hits you in the face, you should turn your head so they can hit the other cheek!"

"No wonder they don't do what Jesus said! That's pretty painful!" Chad hit himself in the face to demonstrate, which made everyone laugh.

"How do you know all this stuff?" asked Vinny, clearly expressing the question on all their minds.

"We're studying it in World Religions class," Matt said casually. *At least I am,* he added to himself.

16

Veras is Right

Tina got up Monday morning feeling no better than she had the night before. She read another chapter in her Bible, but it made no impression on her. When she dressed, she chose a long-sleeved blouse to cover the ribbon on her wrist.

In Calculus, her first-period class, she sat next to Amanda, greeting her with a cheerful hi that was almost convincing. Amanda returned it with no cheer at all. As the teacher droned on about derivatives and logarithmic expressions, Tina fretted about her friend and wondered why she had been so cold.

After class, Tina asked her, "What's bugging you? Have I done something wrong?"

"Of course you have. You're spending all your time with your new friends, acting like I'm not even there."

"*All my time*? You mean last night at the party? 'Manda, I was just being nice to them. I wasn't ignoring you!"

"What*ever*."

Amanda turned and walked away, leaving Tina more confused than before.

Her best friend avoided her the rest of the day and skipped out on the debate at lunch. Danny showed up, but that just made her feel worse. He was friendly but distant, no hug, no playful pats— he knew something was up. To top it all off, few students showed up for the meeting—no new faces, and not a lot of the regulars, either.

When the debate ended, Randy, who had argued the "fact" side, said what she was sure everyone in the room was thinking. "Too bad we had such a small turnout. We should've kept you on the debate committee, Tina—when you were on it, you publicized them better."

That stung. She was the club's star debater, but had asked to bow out of this month's event so she could concentrate on the musical. Feeling guilty about it, she had offered to still handle the publicity for the debate, just like always. But, preoccupied by last week's rehearsals, she hadn't posted the fliers until Friday morning.

She scrambled to think up an excuse, but the bell rang, clearing out the room, leaving her with only enough time for a meek "sorry." Maria grabbed her at the door.

"Look," she said, as she held up the ribbon on her short-sleeved arm. Tina smiled and pulled back her sleeve to reveal her own. "I prayed for you this morning."

It was the first kind word Tina had heard all day. "Thank you," she replied, but she wanted to hug her instead.

In her next class, English Literature, the teacher read a short story to the class. It was about a father, staring through a kitchen window at his little girl playing in the backyard.

"I was her hero, her refuge, her knight in shining armor. She was my pride, my prize, my fairy princess come to cheer me—"

Tina slipped from the room, unexcused, and hid out in a lavatory stall. The bell rang a few minutes later, followed by the rush of girls in and out of the restroom.

Hoping to avoid running into classmates from her English Lit class, who would surely ask her why she had run out of the room, Tina waited until the tardy bell rang, tried to fix her makeup, then ran to her last class. She was surprised when Ms. Veras said nothing about her late arrival. The teacher typically gave latecomers a hard time, greeting them with her standard, "Thank you for joining us!"

Yet Veras gave Tina nothing but a curious look, then gave the class a ten-minute reading assignment. "And I should think I would see some demonstration of your appreciation. After all, I'm giving up valuable class time for this reading, instead of assigning it over the weekend as I should have."

The class took her cue and applauded, whistled, and pounded their desks. "Thank you, you are *too* kind," she said, bowing before her students. "Now quiet down and crack those books."

Tina opened her textbook and pretended to read. Peering through her hair, she spotted the teacher walking down Tina's row, smiling at the students who bothered to look up. Tina kept her head down, unwilling to give Veras a chance to read the trouble in her puffy eyes. As the teacher walked past her, she felt a gentle squeeze on her shoulder.

She knows, Tina thought. *She knows I'm miserable. She knows she was right.*

17

Jacob's Ladder

Tina dashed from the classroom the moment the bell rang and headed straight for her car, praying that she wouldn't run into anyone she knew. Fifty feet from safety she heard someone call her name. *Ignore it.*

"Tina—wait up!" the voice repeated, louder.

She turned but kept walking. It was Jacob, and somebody with him. They ran to her.

"I wanted to introduce you to my friend Reggie," said Jacob when they had caught up to her just as she reached the car.

Tina dug through her coat pockets in a frantic search for her keys. "Hi, Reggie."

"Hi, Tina," Reggie replied. "Nice to meet you."

"What's the matter?" Jacob asked. "Lose your keys?"

"Yes—No! I left them in my purse. And I left my purse in my locker! And it's starting to rain!" Her voice broke, and she turned her head away from the two boys and slumped against the side of the car.

She felt a hand on her arm. Jacob spoke softer this time. "My car's just over here—let's get inside till the rain lets up."

A moment later, Tina was in the passenger seat, her head in her hands. Reggie climbed into the back while Jacob started the engine and adjusted the heater. The two guys were silent, apparently waiting for her to stop crying.

Tina wiped back her hair. "Sorry to do this to you. Reggie, you must think I'm an idiot."

"Naw, just figured you were having an awful day."

"You got *that* right," Tina shot back.

Jacob dug under the seat, pulled out some clean paper napkins and handed them to Tina. "Wanna talk about it?"

"Got an hour?" she laughed, as she wiped her nose.

"Whatever it takes," Jacob said. "We're all ears."

Tina looked back at Reggie. He put his hands to his ears to make them stick out. She laughed again. "You're too sweet. I'll be all right, really. How about you, Jake? How's the experiment going?" Her own question sounded funny to her. She had never called him Jake before. She rarely called him anything at all. In fact, in the three years they had been in youth group together, they had never had a conversation as long as this one—that is, if she didn't count what their characters said to each other in the play. Now she was sitting in his car, crying.

"I'm doing okay," Jacob replied. "It's tough to remember to ask the question, though. It seems like every other minute, I'm saying or doing something without thinking about it. But actually, I was just telling Reg here about it. That's why I wanted him to meet you."

Tina turned to face Reggie. "Better watch out—this 'What would Jesus do?' business is liable to make you miserable!"

Jacob turned down the heater. "Is that what's got you so upset?"

"In a way—no, make that at least *three* ways—yes, it has!"

"Let's hear them." Jacob's voice was firm yet friendly.

"First, my best friend thinks the whole thing is stupid—and she's jealous because I'm being nice to you guys."

"By *you guys*," asked Jacob, "you mean all us uncool people?"

"No, I didn't mean it like that!"

"Just kidding. What's the second reason?"

"It's just something between Danny and me. I don't want to talk about it."

"Fair enough. What else?"

"It's … too private," Tina stuttered, feeling as if she might cry again. She took a breath and continued. "But I'll tell you another. This whole stupid thing started because I wanted to prove Ms. Veras wrong when she said that if I spent my whole time doing what Jesus would do, *it wood make mee meeserable*." She paused for laughter, but got only smiles. "Then, the first time she sees me after that remark, I'm walking in late to her class, with my eyes all puffy. Then I sit there like a zombie the whole time, never saying a word. She *knew* I was miserable. She knew she was right! I *am* miserable!"

No one said anything for a few seconds, then Reggie broke the silence. "That sounds like *four* ways."

"What! Are you keeping *count*?" she joked, then added, "Stick around, Reggie, I'm sure by tomorrow I'll have four more." This time she wasn't joking.

It got quiet again. Tina rubbed her hand against the fogged up window, suddenly conscious of the awkwardness of the moment, eager for the rain to let up.

Jacob broke the silence. "I think we should pray."

Tina bowed her head and listened as Jacob prayed for her, and then for the rest of the experimenters. When he paused, she added her own prayer. "Lord Jesus, please help me do what you would do, no matter what."

When the prayer ended, quiet Reggie said just one more thing. "I'd like to join your experiment, if that's okay with you."

18

Exposed

On Wednesday afternoon, Matt hung out with his friends at the mall. He was sitting in the food court, sharing french fries with Sarah and Vinny, when Lindy came back from a quick visit to the department store.

"Look what *we've* got," they said in unison, holding out a pair of cheap, matching silver bracelets.

"Those are cool," Sarah said, fondling the jewelry. "How much were they?"

The look-alikes glanced at each other with big eyes. Then Laura laughed and said, "They were *free!*"

"They're giving them away? I want one!" shouted innocent Sarah.

Vinny shook his head. "Sarah, they *stole* them."

Sarah jerked her hand away, disgusted.

Matt was disgusted too. "You guys are—I don't believe you did that! Take them back!"

"Why should we?" Laura protested. "That store's just a big rip-off anyway. They jack up their prices, and the owners get rich while the employees get paid squat. I should know—I worked there last summer!"

"And weren't they the ones that got sued last year for not hiring enough African-Americans?"

asked Vinny. "Don't you remember that big thing in the news?"

"So what? Does that make it okay to steal from them?"

"Yes, Matt!" Cindy insisted. "It does! If they're going to rip people off, break the law, and get rich at other people's expense, then we even the scales a bit."

"Kind of like Robin Hood!" the other Lindy added.

"It's nothing like Robin Hood," Matt scoffed. "It just makes you as bad as them. I thought you were better than that. Quit trying to rationalize, and take those things back!" Matt had never stood up to Lindy before. They were a year older and a lot quicker with the tongue. But this time they had gone too far.

"Why, Matthew?" Laura taunted. "Because that's what *Jesus* would do?"

Matt was stunned into silence.

"I don't get it," said Sarah, after a short pause. "What's Jesus have to do with it?"

Cindy answered, "It seems Matthew here is becoming a Jesus Freak."

"I am not! Who told you that?"

"My sister is best friends with Victoria," answered Laura. "You know, Victoria in your *World Religions class*?"

"So what?" He was trying to sound angry, but it came out mad-but-scared.

"She said you were part of an experiment. She said you agreed to be a Jesus Freak for two weeks."

"That's not it at all! The *assignment* was to act *like* a Christian—not *be* one!"

"I don't get it," Sarah said. She looked at Matt with genuine curiosity.

Sarah didn't know how to be mean—one of the many traits Matt loved about her. He directed his answer to her, explaining that all he had to do was make decisions according to what Jesus would do— which meant to be nice, respect people, tell the truth. "It's no big deal. I can just do what I normally do, find junk from the Bible to back up my actions, then stand up in class next Friday and tell everyone that I acted just like Jesus and, by the way, *I'm an atheist.*"

"So *that's* why you wouldn't help us on Saturday!" exclaimed Laura.

"Of *course*. Now I get it!" her look-alike joined in. "How *could* you get us those CDs on your discount? That would mean lying or cheating, or even *stealing*—and we all know *Jesus* would never do that!"

"I don't get it," Sarah complained. "What's she talking about, Matt?"

This time Matt ignored her.

Cindy seemed to give in. "Well, if it will make you feel better, we'll take back the bracelets—"

"*Back home with us!*" said Laura, finishing the taunt.

Matt just shook his head, got up, and walked away.

19

Showdown

Danny showed up at Tina's house at six o'clock Friday night, dressed in a sharp gray suit. Tina met him at the door, wearing a blue dress that she'd bought especially for their big anniversary date. Her folks were there, and her mom insisted on taking pictures of the "happy couple."

"Don't worry," Tina whispered in Danny's ear, after they had been blinded by the flash several times, "she'll run out of film eventually!"

As they drove away in Danny's just-washed truck, Tina asked, "Okay, enough with the suspense! Where are we going?"

"Dinner, silly," was all he replied, with his favorite grin.

It turned out to be a feast, at an expensive Italian restaurant where the food came in courses. Danny looked startled by the bill, but when she offered to chip in, he said, "No way—this is *my* treat." He seemed so pleased with himself, she didn't argue. After paying the check, he pulled out an envelope and set it before Tina. She opened it to find a card—and two tickets to a play she had been talking about for months. She screamed in joyful surprise, then giggled in embarrassment when everyone in the restaurant turned to look.

"Tonight?"

"Yep. So let's get going—we don't want to be late!"

She laughed and cried from the edge of her seat through the whole performance. Danny seemed to enjoy it too, or at least he seemed to enjoy watching Tina have such a fine time.

On the way home, Danny drove them to the park at the lake—a spot they had visited many times in their six months together. Tina talked excitedly about the performance; Danny listened quietly as he stared at the city lights dancing on the ripples of the lake. The radio was playing low, too low to make out the songs. But when Tina had finished her praises for the play, she noticed the music and shut off the stereo.

"Hey, I like that song," Danny objected—his first words since he had shut off the engine.

"It sounds sad. I don't feel like being sad right now."

Danny leaned over and draped his arm across her shoulder. "I'm glad you had a great time tonight. And it's nice to see the old Tina come out again. I was starting to worry about you this week. What's going on with you and Amanda?"

"I don't really know. I guess she's upset because I've been spending time with others lately. But when I make an effort to spend time with her, she avoids me."

"I know the feeling."

That was the door Tina had been waiting for. She knew she had to bring up the subject of their physical relationship. The evening had been too full and too fun to interrupt with that conversation. Now was her first and best opportunity. But how would he react? Would he understand? Did he feel guilty too? Maybe he'd be relieved. Or maybe he'd get mad. The more she thought about it, the more she feared opening her mouth. Maybe it could wait.

But Danny didn't want to wait. "Tina, is everything okay between us?"

She hesitated. "Yeah—I guess so."

"That sounds reassuring! What do mean, you *guess* so? What's wrong?"

There was no way out. He was looking at her, but in the dim light she couldn't make out his expression. "You know the experiment I'm doing for Veras's class?"

Danny sighed. "The famous experiment. Yes, believe me, I know it."

"Well, it's made me ask some questions about our relationship. Our physical relationship."

She stopped there, waiting for him to respond. His face turned, his arm on her shoulder got lighter, but he said nothing.

Tina continued, speaking more softly. "What we're doing—do you think it's what Jesus would do?"

"That's a dumb question. Of course not. Jesus didn't have a girlfriend!"

"But if he did—if he were in your shoes, would he do what we do?"

"Tina, it's not like we're sleeping together." His voice sounded harsh and loud coming right after hers. "We just express our love for each other . . . well, *personally*. You do love me, don't you?"

She'd heard that line before, from Kevin. *Please, God,* she prayed, *don't make this turn out that way.* She reached over to grab his other hand from the steering wheel. "You know I do, but I'm just not sure that it's right to express that love the way we do. I'm not sure Jesus would, anyway. Otherwise, I wouldn't be feeling guilty."

"You're taking this Jesus thing too far. He was perfect. Besides, we both know plenty of Christians who go a lot further. I think Jesus would be pleased that we're not like them."

"Maybe so. But how about other people? How would your mom and dad feel if they knew what we did? How about Pastor Jim?" She shuddered at that picture—imagining how her parents and youth minister would react if they found out what their "ideal couple" were up to.

Danny let go of her hand and grabbed the wheel again. "It's none of their business! It's my life— and what I do with it is between me and God."

But what about my life? Tina thought.

Danny took his arm from her shoulder and gripped the wheel with both hands. "So what are you saying? Do you want me to stop being physical with you? Do you want me to just shake hands?"

"That's not what I'm saying!" She heard anger in her voice and paused to lower the tone. "But I do think we need to draw a line."

"A line. With a big sign that says DO NOT CROSS! Okay, where do you want to draw this line?"

Tina told him. He said he couldn't believe she was being so strict. She tried to explain about her feelings of guilt. He argued, she pleaded, he objected. She told him it had to be that way; he accused her of dissecting their great relationship. She said that it wasn't a great relationship, according to Jesus, and needed fixing. He asked her to respect his "needs"; she asked him to respect her beliefs.

"So what you're telling me is that you just want to be *friends*."

"No, *boy*friend and *girl*friend." She was still pleading—with tears now. He was still arguing.

"What's the point? You've taken the *boy* and *girl* parts out of it. All we're left with is *friends*." Danny started the engine and jammed the truck into reverse. "And I've seen how you treat your friends."

20

Lunch Crew

The ringing phone drove Tina's heart into her throat. She let it ring a few times, preparing for what she would say to Danny.

"Hello?"

"Hi, Tina, this is Jacob. You okay? Sounds like I just woke you up."

Her heart sank when she heard his voice. "No— I'm up. Just moving slow on a Saturday morning. What's up? It sounds like you're at a party."

"I am, kind of. Remember my friend Reggie? Last night he asked the question—What would Jesus do?—and the answer he got was to make lunches for those homeless people in the park downtown. So he called to tell me about it, and I called Marie and Mitch and a few others. I tried calling you too, but your mom said you were out on a date. Anyway, now there's a bunch of us at Reggie's house, making peanut butter and jelly sandwiches and stuff."

Tina was having a hard time understanding him above all the sounds of laughter and conversation and kitchen noises at his end. "It sounds fun, Jake. So is that why you called? I mean, to tell me about what you and Reggie are up to?"

"Oops! I left out the important part. Can you join us downtown today to hand out the lunches?"

"I guess. Yes, I'll come."

She had fallen asleep last night still angry at Danny—at his selfishness, his cutting words, his stubborn refusal to even consider that what they were doing physically might be wrong.

She'd still been angry when she woke up this morning—not at Danny, but at herself. How could she have been so stupid? She had spoiled a good thing, crashed a relationship that was the envy of all her friends. And all because of a silly promise— a promise made to Ms. Veras just to prove her wrong. So what if she won her argument with Ms. Veras? It wasn't worth losing Danny over. Maybe she would call him when she got home. Maybe she could fix things, tell him she was wrong, ask him for some kind of compromise.

But there was still that question: What would Jesus do? And the promise she'd made in front of Jacob and Reggie—to act like Jesus, *no matter what*. Just this morning, in her quiet time—a regular activity since last weekend—she'd been reading John's sixteenth chapter and had stumbled on Jesus' words: "I tell you the truth, you will weep and mourn while the world rejoices. You will grieve, but your grief will turn to joy." She was doing plenty of grieving now—those she counted on and cared most for were abandoning her left and right. Her father. Amanda. And now Danny. When would it all turn to joy? And how *could* it? Joy seemed a million miles away, and the distance made the grieving that much more painful.

Tina drove her mom's van downtown and parked across the street from the dingy park. The homeless men, and a few women too, were scattered about the park, sitting on benches, napping beneath the naked trees, or conversing in clumps on the winter-brown grass, their belongings arranged about them in plastic bags and backpacks and rusty shopping carts.

The lunch crew was there too, easy to spot in their clean clothes, carrying cardboard boxes filled with paper sacks. They had arranged themselves into groups of twos and threes, each group located in their own corner of the park. Tina spotted Jacob and Reggie, Mitch and Maria among the dozen or so kids. But who were all the others?

"Hello there, young lady." Tina heard the old man say as she came upon Reggie and Jacob. He had a full head of greasy black hair, a gaunt face, and wore layers and layers of dirty, mismatched clothes. He was leaning on a broken-down shopping cart filled with sacks of junk. "Have some of these cookies. You look like you could use some cheering up."

Was it really that obvious? She had been working hard to appear cheerful, but her fretting about last night's events had seeped into her smile. "Thanks, but no."

When the two boys refused too, the man immediately inhaled the treats he had been so willing to share, contrasting them kindly to the "sad excuse for cookies they serve at the rescue center." Then he gave Jacob a long, curious look. "You remind me of my son—he must be seventeen by now."

"When did you last see him?" Tina asked, her voice soft.

The man turned to wave to someone coming across the seat. "Dunno. Maybe four, five years."

"Do you miss him?" She regretted the question as soon as she'd said it. She had no right to pry.

His head was still turned; she couldn't tell how he would take her question, or if he had even heard it. Just when she was convinced—to her relief—that the old man had missed her question, he turned and looked straight into her eyes. "Yep. But he don't miss me, I'm sure. Who would?" Then he thanked them for the lunch and walked away, pushing his shopping cart before him.

When he was out of earshot, Jacob whispered, "How could I look like his *son*? He looks old enough to be my grandfather!"

When the lunch sacks were gone, Tina followed her companions back to Reggie's car. Soon the rest of the crew joined them, talking excitedly, and sometimes sadly, about the people they had met. Tina felt shy around so many strangers, and when Jacob walked to the other side of his car to get something, she followed him and asked, "Who are all these people?"

"That's Carla, Maria's little sister," he whispered back, pointing to a younger girl busy telling the others how she had prayed in Spanish with a Mexican woman in the park. "And the girl next to her is her friend Rhoda—they're in the junior high group at our church. The two next to Reggie are friends from his church—Tom and Emily. They joined the experiment Wednesday night at Reggie's Bible study! And that kid there," Jacob continued, pointing to a short blond-haired guy near Mitch, "he's Mitch's cousin. He's not even a Christian."

Jacob pulled a notepad from the car and walked back to the group, leading Tina with him. In a pause in the conversation, Jacob announced, "Hey, everyone, I want you all to meet Tina. She's the one who started this whole experiment."

Tina blushed at the introduction. And as the strangers introduced themselves to her, she felt awkward and proud and humbled, all at the same time. *I didn't do this*, she thought. *This is bigger and better than anything I could ever do.*

Reggie interrupted the introductions. "Jacob and I have already decided that this is something we should do again *next* weekend—something that Jesus would do again."

"If you'd like to join us," Jacob added, "put your name, phone number, and email address on this notepad."

"Can we invite more friends?" asked Carla.

"Of course!" exclaimed Reggie.

"Better watch what you say," laughed Maria. "Carla *tiene muchas amigas!*"

I used to have lots of friends too, Tina thought, then swallowed her self-pity as she saw Maria give her little sister a hug. Carla had one of Maria's homemade ribbons on her wrist.

21

Guinea Pigs

As the lunch crew made their plans for next weekend, Tina quietly excused herself. Handing out lunches to homeless people had been a welcome distraction from her thoughts about Danny. If nothing else, it had put her face-to-face with people more miserable than herself. But making plans about next weekend seemed unreal to her. She couldn't comprehend what life would be like so far in the future. Figuring out how she would face Danny at church tomorrow—and everyone at school next week— was as far ahead as she could see.

Too much to think about. Right now she had some shopping to do. Tina spotted the record store down the block and went there to pick up the CD she knew Michael wanted for his birthday. *Lucky kid,* she thought, knowing that her step-brother had a birthday party at his mom's house today and another at his dad's tonight.

Tina spotted Matt Chen at the register the moment she walked through the door. He saw her at the same time, giving her that special nod that says, "I know you from school, but you're not a friend." She returned the nod and walked past him, then strolled down the aisles looking for the CD.

There was no one else in there—just Matt and her. When she'd found what she came for, she took it to the register. Matt rang up the sale and gave her change for the twenty she handed him, all without saying a word. But as he put the CD in the bag, he broke the uncomfortable silence.

"So you're the other guinea pig in World Religions class." He spoke softly, barely loud enough to be heard above the music playing in the store. Tina realized that it was the first time he had ever spoken to her.

"Yeah, I guess so," she said offhandedly, then asked, "How's it going with your assignment?" It seemed like the polite thing to say, although she doubted he was taking it seriously. How could he, if he was an athcist?

"Okay. But I'm confused about some of the stuff I'm reading for it."

"What are you reading?" She couldn't figure out what *reading* had to do with the assignment. It wasn't a research project. It was an experiment in *behavior*.

"You know, some of the stuff in the Bible."

Tina was embarrassed. Of course he would have to read the Bible if he didn't know anything about Jesus. "What's confusing?"

"Like what are all those little numbers in the paragraphs? They look like footnotes or something, but there aren't any notes for them."

"Little numbers? Oh, I know—those are the verse numbers."

"What are they for?"

"Well . . . when someone quotes something from the Bible, they use those numbers to tell you where they found the verse. So you can look it up yourself, I guess."

"Then what do the other numbers mean—the big ones at the start of each section?"

"Those are chapter numbers."

"My Bible—I mean, the one I'm reading— doesn't have chapter numbers. Just names like Matthew and Mark and stuff. But the chapters are divided up with numbers."

"Oh, I get it. No, what you're calling chapters are really *books*—there are sixty-six of them. Each book is divided into *chapters*—the big numbers you're talking about. And each chapter is divided into *verses*—the little numbers. I know it sounds complicated, but it makes it easier to find your way around."

Tina was going to continue, but a woman stepped into the store. "Many customers while I was at lunch?" the woman asked, stepping behind the counter.

"Two or three," Matt replied.

"Looks like it's going to be a slow day. Mind taking the rest of the day off?"

"Naw, that's cool." Matt grabbed his army coat from under the register and followed Tina out the door.

Standing on the sidewalk in front of the store, Matt thrust his arms through the coat and said, "Thanks for the help—you must think I'm pretty stupid not to know that stuff."

"No—not at all. If you have any more questions, I can try to answer them too. Right now if you like," she added, thinking that anything was better than sitting at home, fighting the urge to call Danny.

Her fellow guinea pig looked down at the pavement and said, "Well, yeah, I do, but . . . well, I haven't eaten anything today, and I'm kind of hungry."

"Me too. We can eat and talk. But only if you want to."

Matt pointed to the deli a few doors down. Tina nodded and followed him. After all, having lunch with this strange atheist Antee was probably something Jesus would do.

22

Exhibit A

Matt munched on his sandwich as Tina sipped at spoonfuls of hot soup. He stared out the window next to them, trying not to focus on her reflection in the glass. He wondered what his friends would say if they walked past, spotting these two opposites having lunch together. The Antee and the Jesus Freak. The sophomore and the senior. The rebellious atheist and the squeaky clean Christian. That picture pleased him—strange, unacceptable, rebellious.

He was surprised and pleased at his own courage. It took guts to ask these questions that would only prove he was ignorant of the Bible. And it took even more guts to sit here and have lunch with her. At school, he would never have done it. She was too popular, too attractive, too perfect. She could be talking and laughing with friends, turn her head to see you, then look right through you like you didn't exist. But that wasn't the same Tina who'd walked into the record store today. Her clothes were ordinary today, she wore no makeup, her hair wasn't perfect—she looked less intimidating, more friendly, approachable. When she had spotted him behind the counter, she'd looked *at* him, not through him, and even smiled. For the first time, Tina Lockhart looked—well—*real*. That's what gave him the courage to ask for help.

"So what else you want to know?" Tina asked, breaking the silence.

He had a dozen questions about what he had been reading, but found it hard to think of them. "Well, I was reading this one chapter—I mean book—called Matthew—"

"Hey, you've got your own book in the Bible!"

"Yeah, that's what made me read it first. But anyway, right after that book, there's another book called Mark, and a couple of others, and they all seem to be saying the same stuff."

"Those are the four *Gospels*—that word means *good news*."

"But why are there four books telling the same thing? Why write the same stuff over and over?"

"I never thought of it like that. Seems kind of strange. But they tell different stories sometimes. I guess it's kind of like flipping channels on TV, catching the news on different stations. Even though they may be covering the same story, sometimes they cover different parts of the story. Matthew, Mark, Luke, and John—the four Gospel writers— were like newscasters, telling the news about Jesus."

"Then what are all those other books for?"

"Most of the Bible is made up of the Old Testament—those books talk about things that happened before Jesus was born. Then there's the New

Testament. That section starts with the four Gospels—telling what happened when Jesus was on earth. All the books that come after that talk about what happened after Jesus left—including what Christians are supposed to act like nowadays."

"And Christians are supposed to do everything the Bible says?"

"Well—yeah, I suppose. Seems like a lot of stuff, doesn't it?"

Matt nodded his head. "And you believe all that stuff—the miracles and that part about Jesus coming back to life?"

"Yes. That's what it means to be a Christian."

Matt wanted to ask if she didn't think it was stupid to believe that all the miracles in this far-fetched story were really true, but he took a big bite of sandwich instead. With his mouth full, he thought of a friendlier question. "So how are you doing with the assignment? It must be pretty easy for you."

Tina looked out the window. At first he thought she hadn't heard him through all the food, but she seemed agitated, like he had struck a nerve or something. He noticed her fiddling nervously with a ribbon on her wrist. After a long pause, she said, "It seems pretty weird, you know."

"What's weird?" replied Matt, worried that he had just said or done something wrong.

"That we're sitting here. You're an Antee—and an atheist, if what Mitch says is true."

He nodded, but she wasn't looking.

"And I'm a Christian, and I'm supposed to be showing everyone that being a Christian is cool and fun and better than . . . well . . . *not* being a Christian. So I *should* tell you that the experiment is going just perfect, and doing what Jesus would do is simple and makes my life better than ever. But if I did *tell* you that, I'd be lying, and that's not something that Jesus would do. So instead, I'll tell you the truth. It sucks."

Matt couldn't believe his ears. Here was this smart, pretty, outspoken Christian, who had made such a big deal about her faith so many times in Veras's class, eating her own words. Inside, part of him was cheering—there's nothing quite like watching an arrogant opponent admit defeat. But the cheering died quickly as he looked at the person on the other side of the table. This was definitely *not* the Tina Lockhart he had seen at school. The girl sitting across from him was being totally honest, totally real—even though doing so made her look bad.

"I'm kind of glad to hear you say that—"

"I figured you would be," Tina interrupted, as she turned to look at him. "Now you can tell all your friends that Christians—or at least, this Christian is a big fat hypocrite."

He shook his head. "I wouldn't do that," he reassured her, surprised to find that he actually meant it. "The reason I'm glad to hear it is that I've been having a really tough time too. I try to be honest with people, but it just gets me in trouble. I try to respect them, but they don't respect me back. No wonder those people murdered Jesus—everything he said and did seemed to tick people off!"

"If that's what it means to act like Jesus—doing things that tick people off—I must be doing pretty well!" She looked like she was trying to smile, but couldn't.

"So if things are so bad, why don't you just tell Veras you don't want to do it?" He was thinking of doing that very thing on Monday—even if it meant a lower grade and another confrontation with his dad.

"I can't—I told some kids at my church about it, and they made the commitment too. How would it look if I quit? I'm the one who started it!"

"You mean there are others going through this—and not even for extra credit?"

"Hard to believe, isn't it? But I'm glad they're gluttons for punishment, because right now, they're about the only friends I've got left. How about you? If you don't mind my asking, why did *you* volunteer?"

"I need the extra credit. If I don't pull up my grades, my dad will crucify me. So I guess either way, I'll find out how tough it is to be like Jesus."

After lunch, Tina offered him a ride home. As the two walked past the park on the way to her car, a shabby old man turned and waved at Tina. She waved back. Matt didn't ask.

Matt climbed into the passenger seat and told her where he lived. Tina pushed a tape into the stereo. As Tina pulled into the street, he tried to figure out which band they were listening to. Working in the record store, he heard all types of music and could identify just about any band. But he was sure he'd never heard this one—and he liked their sound a lot. So he asked.

"Never heard of them," he replied, when she named the band.

"Like them?"

"Yeah, they're not bad."

Tina ejected the tape and handed it to him. "Here. Borrow it."

They didn't say much else on the short drive to his house. Matt was still trying to figure out who this Tina was—the *real* Tina, the Tina who had been so honest and kind, the one who spoke the truth. Over the past week, he had read about Jesus almost every day, scouring the "Gospels," as Tina called them, searching for things he and Jesus could agree on. But the Jesus he read about in those stories was a myth. The person sitting next to him was the real thing.

23

Sunday

She wasn't looking forward to Sunday school. Danny would be there—Danny, to whom she hadn't spoken since their awful parting Friday night. She had hurried home after dropping Matt off Saturday, hoping to find that he had called. No message. Then she'd checked her email, praying that he would have sent an apology, telling her that he had reconsidered and decided that she was right, that they needed to work things out between themselves and God.

No email.

At Sunday school, she would also run into Amanda. And Amanda would catch her talking with the other experimenters and get even angrier. Unless, of course, Tina ignored the other experimenters, which would violate her experiment. She considered skipping church that morning, telling her folks that she wasn't feeling well, which was true enough— she felt sick in the heart. But her morning quiet time—a regular activity since last weekend— reminded her of the question, "What would Jesus do?" Well, he surely wouldn't run from his problems. He'd face them, conquer them. As she finished her Bible reading in John 16, she heard Jesus encouraging her: "I have told you these things, so that in me you may have peace. In this world you will have trouble. But take heart! I have overcome the world."

So she went to church, praying that she might have peace in Jesus, even if she couldn't have it in the troubling world around her.

When Tina stepped into the senior high room, she looked for Amanda and Danny among the other seniors congregating in the back, but they hadn't shown up yet. That was a relief. As she walked toward that group, she saw Paul, Danny's best friend, glance at her and then whisper something to the others, who looked up and stopped talking.

In all her thinking all weekend long about Danny and what it would be like to see him that morning, she had never considered the likelihood, now obvious, that he would tell Paul about Friday night, and Paul would tell others, and soon everyone else would know.

She panicked, turning away to find refuge among Maria, Jacob—even Mitch. She spotted her fellow experimenters at the other end of the room and ran for cover. As she approached, she could hear them telling the small group around them about their adventures downtown on Saturday. Mitch invited everyone listening to join them next Saturday to do it again. Some were interested, others said they'd "think about it."

Pastor Jim bustled in and called everyone to their seats, and as Tina sat down, Maria plopped down next to her. "Guess what?" Maria exclaimed in a loud whisper. "After we got home from downtown, my little sister called a couple of her friends to tell them about the lunch crew and the experiment and everything, and they want to join us too! Is it okay if junior highers are a part of it?"

"Of course," Tina whispered back.

"I kind of figured it was, so I told Carla to bring her friends over after the lesson to join us for a prayer. Are you sure it's okay?"

"I'm sure."

As Jim started the lesson, Tina marveled at her own change in attitude. Months ago, when Jim had asked the youth group's leadership team if they felt it was okay to let junior highers try out for parts in the musical, she had voted against it. "They're too immature," she had complained, before the vote was taken. But after observing Carla's gentle boldness with the homeless on Saturday, she figured that acting like Jesus was a thing that didn't depend on age.

Besides, she needed all the prayers she could get.

Danny and Amanda came in five minutes late, sneaking into chairs at the back. Apparently, they hadn't seen Tina. At least they didn't return her glance when she spotted them.

After the lesson, Jacob wove his way among the departing students to ask each of the experimenters to stay for a few minutes. Apparently, he and Maria had planned some kind of meeting. Tina was actually relieved—it gave her an excuse to avoid her best friend and her ex-boyfriend. Carla and her junior high friends came in a moment later, joining the rest of them at the front of the room.

Maria had mentioned that her sister had recruited a "couple" of friends. But counting Carla and her friend Rhoda from the lunch crew, there were *six* junior highers, all quiet and serious-looking, aware that they had entered a sacred room normally off-limits to them.

But they did not outnumber the senior highers, whose ranks had grown too, to Tina's surprise. *Apparently,* she thought, *the others have been recruiting their friends—while I've been busy losing mine.*

Jacob took charge of the meeting, welcoming the new experimenters and asking people to introduce themselves. After that, he briefly explained the history of the experiment—Tina's classroom assignment, how he and the others had joined her, and their promise to do what Jesus would do no matter what. He was starting to ask if the new students were willing to make that promise when Tina interrupted.

"I think I should say something. Before you make that promise, I should warn you what it might mean. As Jake said, this started out as a classroom assignment. I suggested it to the teacher because I wanted to prove to her and everyone else in the class how great it was to be a Christian. You know, stand up and demonstrate that Christians have it all together. Or, at least, that *I've* got it all together. The truth was, I wanted to put the teacher in her place for being so down on our faith. Instead, it's like the teacher is putting me in *my* place. Or more like God is. When I ask what Jesus would do, sometimes I can't even deal with the answer. What Jesus would do can sometimes be too tough to handle. So be careful what you promise," she warned, as she looked up from the floor to see if people were still listening. They were, and with a kind of respectful attention she had seldom received before. No need to tell them about her breakup with Danny—judging from the compassionate looks she was getting, it was clear that most of them already knew.

No one said anything, so Tina got bolder and asked, "Some of you who are new to this promise thing. What made you decide to do it?"

It was quiet for a bit, then one of the junior guys said, "It just seems like the right thing to do." Others nodded in agreement.

Carla jumped in. "Yesterday, when I saw how all you guys were working together to serve lunches to those poor people downtown—I don't know, I guess I just wanted to be that way with my own friends."

"I've watched how Maria and you have been acting at school," said Kaylyn, a junior girl whom Tina barely knew. "I want to act that way too."

"I can understand your wanting to be like *her*," Tina offered, giving Maria a shoulder hug, "but I'm afraid I'm not much of a model of what Jesus is like."

"But you are," said Patricia, another new person and Kaylyn's friend. "Jesus went through tough times too—and he didn't give up. We've seen you at school. And we've seen that you're different now—even though you're obviously going through some junk that's pretty awful."

Tina managed a smile. "Well, the good news is, it can't get much worse, so why give up just when it might get better!"

Jacob asked everyone to huddle up for prayer. As they linked arms and bowed their heads to pray, Tina saw another huddle in the back of the room. Jim and the adult leaders were praying too. Jim looked up at the same moment and returned her smile. It was more than an acknowledgment that they'd both been caught peeking in prayer. His smile said, "We're praying for *you*."

Walking out to the parking lot, Tina remembered what she'd read in the Bible that morning. Maybe it was true. Maybe the grief *would* turn to joy. Jesus had conquered the world, and in him, she would conquer her troubles.

She spotted Danny driving away in his truck. Amanda was sitting next to him.

24

Our Father

When the customer brought the CD to the checkout counter, Matt didn't recognize the album, but he knew the band's name. It was on the tape Tina had given him the day before. After ringing up the sale, he asked the woman where she'd found the CD.

"In the Christian section," she replied.

He knew they had such a section—a small one, back in the corner between the foreign-language albums and the comedy CDs. But he had never browsed through it, for obvious reasons. When the last customer left that evening, he rifled through the selection and found the same album the customer had purchased.

When he took the CD to Kathy so he could buy it with his discount, he knew just what his manager would say. She didn't disappoint his expectations. "Really, Matthew, I didn't know you were a Christian!"

"I'm not!" he denied, a bit too heatedly.

"Take it easy! I just thought that, since you're buying a Christian album—"

He cut her off. "Listening to that kind of music doesn't make you a Christian. Besides, it's for a

118

school assignment." That last part just barely squeaked by with his "tell the truth" promise.

"Whatever you say."

Matt paid for the CD and stuffed it into his army jacket, feeling the same kind of shame he had felt that day back in eighth grade when he had been caught shoplifting.

At home that night, he listened to his new CD as he played on his computer. But Kathy's accusation—and his reply—were haunting him. What he'd said had been right—listening to Christian music didn't make him a Christian. Nor did reading the Bible, which he had been doing on and off all week to get ready for his report. For that matter, acting like Jesus didn't make you a Christian either. He was doing his best to act like that ancient character, but he was still an atheist.

So what *did* make you a Christian? Tina had said something about believing what the Bible said. That meant believing in a myth, which was stupid. Sure, there was good stuff in there. And if you believed that Jesus was right about most of what he said and did—there was nothing wrong with that. But to believe *everything* was impossible.

Especially the stuff about God. How could a guy as smart as Jesus have been so totally wrong about that? Everywhere he went, it was "the Father" this, "heavenly Father" that. Talking about him, praising him, relying on him, giving him all the credit. Even talking *to* him. If Jesus was such a rebel, why did he have to pretend that he relied on *something*—some*one*—so outlandish?

Even if you cut out all the silly miracles (which had to be fictions added after Jesus was dead, just to spice things up), you'd still end up with Jesus himself, believing in "the Father"—the biggest fiction of them all. And if you took all *those* parts of the story out, you'd have almost nothing left.

As Matt thought this through, his ears caught the lyrics driving through the bass beat of the CD:

Our Father, in heaven above
By your name we're called to love
Rule our hearts, be our king
Reign as Lord of everything
You give us food, you make our days
You take our sins, our selfish ways
You gave us Jesus to bring us together
To give us life, now and forever

If Jesus *were* making this Father thing up in his head—no other explanation made sense—he sure had a lot of people fooled. *But not me*, he reasoned. *I just have to* do *the Jesus thing—I don't have to* believe *it*.

25

Sparks

"I'm so sorry!" whispered Kat in second period.

As Tina slipped into third period Chemistry, Craig asked, "What happened?"

"You can do better!" Janise said during the break, patting her shoulder in encouragement.

Tina hadn't told a soul—not her church friends, nor her school friends, nor even her mom. But by noon on Monday, news of her breakup with Danny had rippled across the campus. She spent the day hearing condolences and fending off questions. Some of her guy friends treated her differently, less like a buddy and more like a potential conquest. Maybe they figured that with Danny out of the picture, they'd get their chance.

It was worse with a few of her girl friends. Apparently they had similar visions of themselves with Danny, which meant distancing themselves from his "ex" in the hope of being his "next." But from what she saw and heard, that position was already filled.

She and Amanda managed to say nothing to each other in first period Calculus—which wasn't hard, since the desire to avoid a conversation was mutual. She passed Danny in the hall between classes and made a noble attempt at a kind hello. He returned with a flippant jerk of the head. When the new couple didn't show up at the lunchtime meeting, she was relieved.

It was Tina's turn to lead the meeting, so she had put together a short Bible study last night. The spirit in the room this week contrasted sharply with last week's awful debate. Everyone was talking about the lunch crew adventure Reggie had put together. Actually, Mitch was doing most of the talking, which was no surprise, but what was surprising was the excitement the topic generated. She'd never seen the club so lively. And she had never seen Reggie there either.

The conversation naturally turned to the experiment, with Reggie, Jacob, Maria, and the others telling about their struggles with the dangerous WWJD question. What started out as a casual conversation before the meeting evolved into the meeting itself, as her fellow experimenters told of the decisions they had made and the positive and negative consequences that had followed.

When there were just fifteen minutes left before the bell. Randy called the meeting to order and asked Tina to begin the Bible study. She spoke from the heart instead.

"Unlike last week, I *did* do my homework for this meeting," Tina began, holding up her Bible study notes. "But while the rest of you were talking about doing what Jesus would do, I asked myself that question. So—here goes: First, I'd like to apologize to all of you, and especially to you, Randy, for flaking out with the debate promotion. I was caught up in my own selfish little world, and I let you guys down. I will do my best to promote our next activity.

"And that brings up another thing. I need to ask for your forgiveness for some other things I've done." As Tina paused to muster her courage, she could feel the dead silence in the room. She continued, speaking slower and more softly. "Kaylyn, you said something yesterday after our Sunday school class that went straight to my heart. You said that the way Maria and I acted was the reason you decided to take the promise we were just talking about. I wondered what you could have possibly seen in me that was anything like Maria.

Tina paused and turned to Maria, her voice heavy with emotion. "Maria, you are kind and cheerful, innocent, loving, forgiving, gracious, giving. You've become my friend, even though I've been snobby toward you ever since you came into high school. You made this bracelet for me. You've cheered me up when I've felt like crap. You've prayed for me when your own troubles were even bigger than mine. You remind me of Jesus.

"When Kaylyn put me in the same class as you, I felt ashamed because I'm nothing like you." She turned to face the rest of the group and continued. "I've treated some of you horribly. I pretend that I've got it all together, that I'm living a good Christian life, that I'm a good witness for Jesus. But I'm not. I'm a big fake. It's all a lie. I'm selfish, jealous, and arrogant. I think I'm somehow better than others because I read my Bible and go to church."

Tina paused again. If it were possible, the room was even quieter than before. Maria's eyes were misty, and a few others too, including her own. "I'm sorry for pretending I was something I'm not. I'm sorry for the way I've treated some of you—all of you. I hope you can forgive me. I *want* to be like you, Maria. I want to live up to your view of me, Kaylyn. Most of all, I want be more like Jesus, and less like the person I've been pretending to be."

The next thing Tina knew, she was smothered in Maria's arms, then more arms, then more.

26

Christianity vs. Jesus

The rest of Tina's school day went by in a blur. She recalled nothing that was said in her last two classes—her mind was too full with what had happened at lunch. She had confessed that she wanted to stop pretending, wanted to start acting like Jesus. But what did that really mean? She had always believed that "being a Christian" and "being like Jesus" were just two ways of saying the same thing. Now she wasn't so sure. She was a committed Christian—everyone knew it. But she wasn't much like Jesus. How was it possible to be one thing and not the other?

And what difference did that make to the struggles she was still facing? She felt somehow better for having told the real truth about herself, but that still didn't change the state of affairs with Danny or Amanda—make that Danny *and* Amanda. Nor did it resolve anything with her father. When she'd simply been living as a Christian—rather than as someone who lived as Jesus would—she had been doing just fine in those areas.

Well, no, that wasn't completely true. In her relationship with Danny, even before the experiment, things hadn't been perfect. But at least she'd been *trying* to be a good Christian in that area, and doing a pretty good job at it. Why else had people always been saying that Tina and Danny were the "ideal Christian couple"? Trying to be a good Christian had worked fine for everyone. It was trying to act like Jesus that had doomed their relationship.

The same was true with Amanda. They were best friends—*Christian* friends. Friends who did Christian things *together*. Everything was fine till Tina tried to act like Jesus instead. Did choosing between "being a Christian" and "acting like Jesus" mean choosing between Amanda and Tina's new friends? Why did she have to choose at all?

Then there was her father. How was it possible that this experiment had made things worse between Tina and her father? How *could* it? She hadn't even *seen* him in years! But things *were* worse. As a Christian, she had learned to do without him. To leave the past behind. And to hate what little remained of him in her memory. Hating him wasn't exactly *Christian*—but then again, neither was what he had done to her and her mom. And besides, God understood—or so it seemed, because he had let her hold on to this one little secret hatred, stowed safely inside her where it wouldn't hurt others. Now even that was impossible. Acting like Jesus meant letting go of the hatred. It meant forgiveness. And forgiveness was impossible.

Her lunchtime confession may have wiped the slate clean with those who'd been there. And certainly, she felt a new freedom, a new resolve to act like Jesus in her new life. But nothing had changed with the bigger issues. In those areas, acting like Jesus had *caused* all the trouble. How could doing the same thing *resolve* them?

27

Questions

"Hi, Matt. Did you get a chance to listen to more of that tape?" Tina had caught up with him after World Religions class.

He seemed startled to hear his name—at least to hear it from her. "Yeah, I listened to it. Pretty good. I saw another one of their albums—at the record store."

"Really? I didn't know they had a new one. Maybe I should stop by and get it."

"It's even better, I think. More alternative, if you like that kind of music."

Tina was surprised. Matt hadn't just listened to the tape—he'd gotten hold of *another* album. Did he know that it was a *Christian* band?

Matt continued. "Hey, now I know why you were downtown on Saturday—and why that old man in the park waved at you."

"Yeah? Why was I downtown?"

"Some of my friends told me they saw the Jesus Freaks—sorry, I mean you and your friends—handing out lunches to the homeless people."

"What'd they say about it?" Tina was curious to know what the Antees thought about things.

"Just that you were handing out lunches."

He looked like he was holding back, so Tina kept at him. "Yeah? What else did they say?"

"Well, they did say that you guys looked kind of out of place—but I think maybe they were jealous 'cause they didn't think of it first."

"It doesn't matter *who* thought of it!" Tina laughed. "Anyway, we're doing it again next Saturday—in case you and your friends want to join us."

"That'd be the day!" Matt shuddered. "I can't imagine what it would look like if those two groups got together!"

"It would be almost as weird as us having lunch together!"

"Weirder."

"Hey, if you've got any more questions about the Bible, we can talk about them. If you want."

"I thought of more stuff—you know, things that could help me with my report, but I've got to go to work."

"What time do you get off?" Tina asked, surprised at her own boldness.

"Five."

"Why don't I stop by the record store about then to pick up that album. Then, if you want, we can talk some more."

"Sure—if you want."

* * *

Tina got to the record store a few minutes early, paid for the album, and walked with Matt to the deli. On the way, she prayed. *Please, Jesus, open Matt's heart.*

As they sipped their sodas, Matt asked more questions—the kind of questions that revealed the great amount of reading he had been doing in his Bible. He asked about specific things Jesus had said and done—and *why*. Then he asked about "the Trinity"—a subject they had covered in class that week.

"It doesn't make sense," Matt said, not buying her answer. "If *Jesus* was supposedly God, why did he keep asking the Father for help? If he was really God, he didn't *need* anybody's help. And for that matter, if he was God, and the *Father* was God, why did he pray to him? Wasn't he just praying to *himself*?"

"I wish I had great answers for you, Matt, but I don't. To be honest, it confuses me too."

"But how can you believe in something if it doesn't make sense to you?"

"I guess because enough of it *does* make sense. Just because I don't *understand* it all doesn't mean I should stop *believing* it all."

"Yeah, but why don't you just believe in the realistic stuff, and toss out the ridiculous stuff?"

"What ridiculous stuff?" Tina shot back.

"Well, for one thing, all those miracles. That's like believing in magic."

"Not if you believe that Jesus is really God. If he's God, he can do *anything*."

"But if he could do *anything*, why did he keep going to the Father for help?"

Tina felt frustrated—at Matt for asking all these tough questions, at herself for not knowing all the answers. And at God, for not answering her prayer about softening Matt's heart. Then, as if God had heard her silent complaint, an answer occurred to her—something she had read in John 17.

"It's like this, Matt. When Jesus showed up on earth, he did it to tell people about God. He wanted them to know that there really *was* a God—a God who loved them. He also wanted to show people that there was a right way to live—a way that *pleased* God instead of ticking him off. He said that the number one way to please God was to love and obey him.

"But he didn't just *say* it. He *did* it himself. He didn't just *say*, 'Love God.' He *demonstrated* what it meant to love God—or the *Father*, as Jesus called him. He didn't just *say*, 'Obey God.' He *showed* us what obedience looks like—by obeying the Father himself. Jesus wasn't a hypocrite, saying one thing and doing another. When he said something, he did it.

"So here's the answer to your question: Yes, Jesus *could* have done anything. But to show us an example, he did only what the Father told him to do. He was totally obedient, in everything he said, everything he did."

"You keep saying *obedient*—you make it sound like he was a dog or something."

"No, I don't mean it that way!" Tina objected. "Well . . . I guess, maybe in a way I *do* mean it that way. Jesus obeyed his master—God—to show us that we should obey our master too."

"You mean sit, roll over, play dead."

"No, I mean, 'Heel! Stay by my side!—because if you run into the street, you'll get hit by a car!' God wants us to obey him because he loves us and knows what's best for us. He doesn't want us to get hurt."

"But Jesus didn't *always* act like an obedient dog. He caused a lot of trouble, too. He rebelled against the rules—he didn't obey them."

"That's the whole point! When you obey someone, you *have* to be a rebel against other things. If your friends say, 'Let's go out and party tonight!' and your dad says, 'Stay home!'—you can't obey them both. If you obey your friends, you rebel against your dad. If you obey your dad, you rebel against your friends. Jesus obeyed *his* dad, and sometimes that meant rebelling against other things. And since he *always* obeyed the Father, he wound up being a rebel a lot!"

Matt nodded his head and sucked the last drops of soda from his straw. *Maybe this is making sense!* she hoped. She felt proud of her little speech, proud that she had thought of these things off the top of her head.

"So are you that way, Tina?"

His question took her by surprise. Just like that fateful day in Veras's class, the conversation had turned from "Christianity in general" to "Tina's faith" in a split second. "Am I *what* way?" she asked, hearing the wall go up in her own voice.

Matt leaned forward and spoke earnestly. "Do you follow Jesus' example? Are you obedient to God?"

He wasn't attacking her. It was the question itself that attacked her—the same question that had been haunting her for days. She had told the painful truth to her Christian friends. Now it was time to tell Matt. "No, I'm not. I used to think I was doing pretty good, but lately I'm realizing I'm not even close. Most of the time I *don't* obey. I don't do what Jesus would do."

"But you're a Christian."

"Yeah, but that doesn't mean I act like Jesus. I used to think they were the same thing, but they're not."

Matt nodded and said nothing. For just a moment, Tina thought of explaining the gospel story to him, using a technique she had learned at summer camp. She knew it by heart, having tried it out many times on strangers when the youth group had gone witnessing. But when she pictured Matt as the recipient of her well-rehearsed speech, she knew it was all wrong. He wasn't ready. And when he *was* ready, she'd have to ditch the speech and introduce him to the *real* Tina—the hateful, selfish Tina, the hoarder of secret sins, the one who needed Jesus more than air.

"Got email?" Tina asked as they got up to go. Matt nodded yes, so Tina grabbed a paper napkin and wrote out her address. "If you think of any other questions, send them to me and I'll try to answer. Can I give you a ride home?"

Driving to his house, she remembered something he had said last week. "So how are things with your dad?" she asked.

"Same as always. He's usually upset with me for one thing or another. When he asks about school, I used to lie to him, but then he'd find out anyway and blow up at me. Now I try to tell him the truth—and he *still* blows up. I guess I can't win. How about you? You get along with your dad?"

The question hit her completely off guard. Her feelings about her father had for years been buried deep, untouchable by all but Amanda, and even then, only on rare occasions. The birth-announcement card had changed all that; now those feelings were near the surface, where an innocent question like Matt's could expose them. Tina paused to regain control, then tried to lead Matt down another path.

"My stepdad's pretty cool. We can talk and everything."

"What about your *real* dad?"

Tina flinched. Her detour had failed. Now all she could do was lie about it.

Or tell the truth.

Tina pulled to the side of the street. Ten minutes later, Matt had said not a word, but he knew it all. The divorce, the junior-high graduation, the birthday cards, the baby announcement, even the hatred. She felt relieved, embarrassed, hurt, victorious, proud of her total honesty, ashamed that she had let Matt know her darkest sin. An hour earlier, she had prayed that God would open Matt's heart. Instead, he had opened her own, and nothing but garbage had spilled out.

When she was done, she wiped away the tears and said, "I'm so sorry! I can't believe I just told you all that junk. It's been building up in me all week—all because of this stupid experiment! I feel like I've just thrown up on you. I'm *so* sorry." Tina pulled back into the traffic and quickly drove the rest of the way to his house, eager to end the embarrassment.

Still, Matt said nothing. Tina dared not speak again, figuring it would only make this intensely awkward moment worse. But when she turned onto his street, he spoke up.

"I hate my dad too."

Tina looked. He was staring out the passenger window, but when he turned back toward her, his face was contorted to hold back tears.

28

Big Wednesday

Tina came to Bible study expecting to hear Jim teach. But the youth pastor had different plans: he asked the experimenters to share their stories of doing what Jesus would do.

The stories continued for forty-five straight minutes. Mitch had shared his faith with his cousin. Maria had given to the Salvation Army some money her grandmother had given her for her birthday. Malcolm—*When did he join the experiment?* wondered Tina—had led a friend to the Lord, and the friend was there with him to confirm the story. One of the freshman girls had started a before-school prayer group with a few of the others. And among a bunch of other things, Jacob told everyone what had been happening at Reggie's church—and some kids from *another* church that had heard of the WWJD business and wanted to join.

Tina was awestruck. While she had been fighting battles with her own disobedience—and struggling to survive the consequences—her new friends had been spreading the experiment through three churches, dozens of lives, in homes, schools, and friendships. She said just one thing about her own experiences: "I've been talking about Jesus to someone at school." She didn't tell them who.

When the meeting broke up, Tina saw Amanda and Danny leave. She followed after them, reaching the door when the couple—now arm in arm—were halfway down the hall.

"Amanda, Danny—wait up."

The two flinched like they had just heard a gun shot. They turned to face her. Amanda took a half step away from Danny.

"Before you go," Tina said, trying to tame the quaver in her voice, "I wanted to say something." She took a breath and added, "Wow, this is awkward!"

Amanda said, "Yeah."

Danny just shrugged.

"Look, I know you two are seeing each other. You don't have to hide it from me. I wish I could say it wasn't painful to see you together, but ... well ... it is. There's nothing I can do about that." Then her voice broke, making the next part *sound* painful. "I love both of you—I really do—and if I didn't, I guess it would be easier."

Amanda reached out and hugged her friend. Danny was still standing there, stiff as a soldier, but he reached over and put his hand on Tina's arm.

When they let go, Tina continued. "So the two of you being together—I can live with that. But what I *can't* live with is the thought of our not being friends anymore. The pain of losing you as my friends would be worst of all. I know I've hurt each of you, in one way or another, and I'm sorry for that. I hope we can forgive—at least, I hope you can forgive *me*, and we can somehow get past this awkwardness and be friends again."

This time, both of them hugged her, and she hugged back. When they let go, The couple looked stunned. She rescued them. "I've gotta go. See you at school."

Tina turned and walked back to the senior high room. As she passed through the door, she glanced back to see Amanda and Danny still standing in the hall, in shock. Or was it wonder, or shame—she couldn't tell which.

29

The Last Thing

Tina found Matt's email message when she got home that night:

"Thanks for your help the other day. I didn't mind it when you told me about your dad. I hate it when people act like they're perfect, because they're only lying—no one is perfect. Everybody hurts. Everybody screws up. Everybody bleeds. People who say they don't are just liars. Thanks for telling the truth. I'm sorry it's so painful. You're too nice a person to go through that crap. I wish you didn't have to. I wish there was something I could do.—Matt"

After spilling her guts on Monday, she had been afraid to talk to him. He had said hi to her at school a couple of times, but she was sure he thought she was a basketcase. His message erased her fears. She wrote a reply:

"Matt: You're right—nobody's perfect. Everybody screws up. Even dads. I guess that's why I need Jesus. If things were perfect, I wouldn't need his help. Or yours—thanks for listening to my problems. Write back if I can help you too.—Tina"

After sending her reply, she felt an overwhelming need to pray. Usually her prayers were short and silent—more like thoughts aimed at God than a real conversation. But tonight she spoke them out loud, in a quiet, natural voice, as if God were sitting in front of her, eager to hear every word. She asked God to show himself to Matt—to let him know that he wasn't just a myth. She thanked him for all the great things happening among those who had made the promise, mentioning each person by name. She thanked him for the courage he'd given her—to confess her sins in front of the club members at school, to make peace with Amanda and Danny.

She asked him to guide her as she prepared her report for World Religions—that she'd have the courage to tell the truth, with humility and grace. And she asked him to forgive her for pretending that she had it all together, that she didn't need him every moment of every day.

As her lips fell silent, she felt at peace. It was so delicious she spoke again, to thank God for that too. As soon as she did, the peace disappeared. Something was troubling her. Something still wasn't right. When she opened her eyes, she saw the baby announcement, wedged between some books on her desk.

That was the something—the thing that wasn't right. On Friday afternoon, she would have to stand in front of her classmates and do one of two things: She could lie by telling them that she'd done what she promised. Or she could tell the truth: "In one thing—the most difficult thing—I just couldn't do what Jesus would do."

She knew she couldn't live with either option. She tried to get her heart to consider a third choice: *forgive her father*. But her heart wouldn't let her. Instead, it flooded itself with every angry and hateful thought she had ever had about him. The idea of forgiveness was drowned in the storm of painful memories of the man who had abandoned her.

Tina fell to her knees and begged God for help. She pleaded with him, chanting his name in desperate sobs, asking him to flush out the awful hatred flooding her heart. Slowly, almost imperceptibly, the flood passed. Forgiveness floated to the top. Not forgiveness for her father. It was *God's* forgiveness. He was forgiving *her*.

30

Ambush

The table conversation stopped the moment Matt sat down at the lunch table. "What's going on?" he asked, trying not to sound too concerned. He got no answer. "What is it?" he tried again, "Did I do something wrong?"

"Why don't *you* tell *us*?" answered one of the Lindys.

"Yeah, tell us what it's like to be a Jesus Freak." said the other.

"What do you mean?"

"We heard that you've become a Christian," Vinny said sarcastically. "I guess all this Jesus stuff finally sank in."

"So is Tina Lockhart your *girlfriend* now?" Cindy asked. "Laura's brother saw her giving you a ride home the other day."

"Guys do the strangest things when they're in *love*," Laura added, hugging her look-alike to demonstrate.

"That doesn't mean they're a *couple*." Sarah was trying to stick up for him, but it didn't help.

"That's not the point," barked Vinny. "The point is that you're taking this Jesus stuff way too far. You're an *atheist*, Matt! How could you possibly take this Christianity thing seriously?"

Before Matt could answer, Cindy jumped in. "Maybe he's not an atheist anymore. Maybe he really *is* a Christian now."

"So what if he is? He can believe whatever he wants to. Who are you to judge him?" Sarah could be pretty ditsy sometimes, but when she wanted to, she spoke her mind loud and clear.

Laura shot to Cindy's defense. "She's only trying to *help*, Sarah! If Matt's getting sucked into all that Christian stuff, then we want to make sure he knows what he's doing."

Chad, who hadn't joined in the interrogation, finally spoke. "Shut up, you guys! You're being total jerks. Give the guy a chance to speak! So what's up, Matt? Is what they're saying true?"

The table got quiet, waiting for Matt to reply to the charges. He knew they wouldn't believe his answers. He looked at Sarah, the friendliest face among them, and began.

"I think it's pretty funny—how people make fun of us because of how we dress, how we act, what we believe in. We make a big deal about being rebels—about standing up for our right to say and do what we think. But then we turn around and rip on Christians for standing up for what *they* believe in. I do it all the time.

"I don't believe in their God, but I've got to respect them for having the guts to believe in him themselves. And from what I've read about Jesus, he was more of a rebel than I'll ever be. If more Christians acted like him, they'd put us to shame. I'm sorry if this offends you, but the truth is, except for all the God stuff, Jesus would have been an Antee. So maybe we should lighten up on all the Christian bashing. Some of them may be jerks, but some of us are jerks too. Like me. So does that answer all your questions?"

Matt stood up and looked around the table. Blank stares, all in shock. Except Sarah—she was smiling. "Sarah, you want the rest of my lunch?" He walked away without waiting for a reply.

Back at his locker, he watched his shaky hand as it tried to dial the combination.

31

Preparing to Jump

All morning long, Tina couldn't stop thinking about her dad. She wasn't angry or hateful or even feeling hurt. This was something entirely new. She was scared.

Mostly, she was afraid to let go of this last little thing that kept her father safely in the past. She fantasized what it would be like — how it would feel to let go of her secret history. What would happen? Would the old, awful feelings return? Could she even face him? Could he face *her*? What did he think of her? Was he like that old man at the park, missing his own child, but convinced that the kid was better off not knowing him?

And what about forgiving him? How *could* she? How could she possibly gather up all the junk of the past—everything he'd ever done to her—and toss it out like it didn't matter anymore? It *did* matter. His absence in her life had been devastating and even now changed who she was, how she acted, even what she thought about guys. What he had done was wrong—and no amount of forgetting or forgiving would ever make it right. Forgiving him was not a flippant gesture. It would take time to know she had truly forgiven him. Then maybe even more time before she could tell him.

If she saw him, what *could* she tell him? If she couldn't say, "I forgive you," could she say, "Please forgive *me*"? After all, God wasn't the only offended party in her hatred. The object of that sin had been her father. She had asked God to forgive her. Shouldn't she ask her father? There was something wrong with that, her head told her. How could she ask her father to forgive her of the hatred *he had caused*?

But her heart was right. She was ultimately responsible for her own sin, just as he was accountable for his. If she couldn't forgive him—in time, yes, but not now—could she ask for forgiveness? Yes. She could.

By lunchtime she had a plan—a ridiculous, outlandish, impossible plan. She abandoned it in English Lit. But sitting in Ms. Veras's classroom, imagining what she would say when she gave her report tomorrow—maybe it *wasn't* impossible. Stupid, yes. Totally scary—most definitely. But impossible—no. She saw the now-faded ribbon on her wrist, the one Maria had tied there nearly two weeks ago. (Had it been only two weeks? It seemed like forever.)

What would *Jesus* do?

When the bell rang, Ms. Veras called out, "Matt and Tina, will you be ready to give your reports tomorrow?"

Matt still didn't quite know what he would say in his report, but he nodded. He heard Tina say yes.

Not five steps out the door, Tina grabbed his shoulder and spun him around.

"Remember in your email," she sputtered, all out of breath, "you said you wished there was something you could do for me—about my dad?"

It took him a moment to remember. "Yeah."

"Did you mean it?"

"Yeah, I guess so—but what can I do?"

"It's going to sound crazy!"

She was right. It did sound crazy. But after what had happened to him at lunch, he was ready for anything. Matt ditched his books in his locker, waited while she did the same, and followed her out to the buses. She was running.

32

Going Home

The two experimenters found the bus that went closest to the train station and jumped on just before it pulled away. The train was Matt's idea. In her fantasy plan, Tina had figured on driving the car. It wasn't until she was explaining it to Matt that she remembered her mom had the car for some all-day meeting out of town, and wouldn't be back till late. Too late.

Matt led her off the bus at the closest stop to the station, but they had to run several blocks in the rain to make it the rest of the way. The train was already in the station. They bought their tickets and barely made it aboard in time. In two hours it would reach her dad's town.

They slumped into a pair of seats, wet from the rain, still breathless from the run. Tina looked out the window as her own town disappeared behind them, thanking God that Matt had come along. He had been her last choice, really. Jacob or Maria or even Amanda might have been a wiser pick, but if she had looked but not found them—or worse, if they had said no—she'd have lost her nerve and given up the plan. She had even considered quirky Mitch—but he hadn't shown up for school that day.

As it was turning out, Matt was a wise, if unlikely, choice. He knew the train schedule because his grandparents lived in the same city as her dad. And he'd known which bus would take them near the station. Still, as she looked at this near-stranger sitting next to her, she wondered what he really thought about this foolhardy adventure. What could possibly have made him say yes to it?

For that matter, why was *she* doing it? Was she really ready to see her dad? What would she say? What would *he* say?

What if he weren't home?

A half-hour later, as the train made a short stop in the next town, she still had no answers. She thought of getting off—turning around and going home—but before she turned her doubts into action, the train began moving again.

The doubts returned at every stop. Each station was like a magnet, pulling her to her senses, beckoning her to turn around and go home. And each time the train pulled away again, she felt more foolish, more scared.

* * *

Thirty minutes before their destination, Matt had run out of things to say. He was awkward among strangers anyway, and Tina's strange mood made conversation even more difficult. He knew so little about her; they had almost nothing in common. He tried talking about the assignment, but that seemed only to remind her of what lay ahead. He tried talking about music, but except for the one band she had introduced him to, they had no common favorites.

As they pulled into the last station before their goal, Tina interrupted the long lull in their conversation. "This is a stupid idea. I want to get off!"

Matt didn't know what to say. It was her plan anyway—she could do what she wanted. But they had come so far—maybe she just wanted him to make the decision for her. He wasn't ready for that responsibility. So he passed the decision to someone else. "Well, we can get off if you really want to. But . . . is that what Jesus would do?"

She gave a short, nervous chuckle and replied, "Now *that's* a dirty trick! Of course not! That's why I'm on this stupid train in the first place." As the train came to a stop, loaded passengers, and then slowly started up again, her hands gripped the seat as if they alone were keeping her on the train.

She was still gripping the seat twenty minutes later when the train slowed and then stopped at their destination. Other passengers rose to disembark, and Tina didn't release her grip. Matt knew she really wanted to go through with this, but her fears were standing in the way. He didn't know how to talk her through it—so he *walked* her through it instead. He grabbed her arm and led her off the train. "Do you know where he lives? Can we walk there from here?"

"I don't know!" she whined. "I forgot to bring his address."

"We'll look it up in the phone book," he said, trying to be cheerful while wondering just how well she had thought out this plan. "What's his name?"

Matt stepped into a phone booth and looked it up, scribbling the address on his hand. As Tina slumped into a seat, he ran to the ticket window to ask for directions. "It's on the other side of town," said the woman behind the glass.

Matt trotted back to Tina. "C'mon, we'll take a cab. And we need to hurry—the last train leaves here in two hours. They dove into a cab in front of the station; Matt gave the address. Fifteen minutes later, they pulled up to the small, one-story house whose street number matched the one on his hand.

When the car stopped, he glanced at Tina. She was staring at her hands. "Could you drop us off at the end of the block?" The driver took them another hundred yards and pulled to the curb. "Sure you wanna do this?"

"No—yes. I don't know!" Matt took that as a yes, paying the fare and leading Tina out of the car. As it drove off, he tried to give her courage. "You've come this far. You're almost there." She nodded and took a step in the direction of the house.

As they walked, he tried to make a joke. "If nothing else, you'll have quite a story to tell in your report tomorrow." She laughed just a little, but it was enough. One house away, he asked, "Do you want me to go with you?"

"No, you've done enough already," she said, squeezing his arm. "I think I should do this alone."

"Good luck."

Tina turned up the walk to the house.

33

Dad

When Tina stopped on the porch, she could hear her pulse thumping in her ears. She turned to look for Matt. He was standing on the sidewalk, silently cheering her on.

Her hand shook as she pushed the doorbell. She waited. And waited. "Maybe no one's home," she thought, hoping it was true. But she heard the latch click. The door opened, and a little girl peeked around the edge of the door.

"Is Mr. Lockhart—is your father home?" she asked quietly, recognizing the girl from the picture.

The girl—her half-sister!—turned and hollered, "Dad! There's someone at the door for you!" A few seconds later, the girl's face disappeared and the door opened the rest of the way. The man she hadn't seen in four years stood and stared back at her.

The photo had prepared her for some of the changes in his appearance. He was heavier, grayer, with an ascending forehead whose uppermost reaches had once been buried in hair. But the photo failed her in other ways. He was now much shorter (or she was taller, which came to the same thing). And the lines connecting his eyes to his temples were deep and permanent, like those of her *grand*father.

"Can I help you?" he asked in a polite and formal voice. Then, in another voice, "Mar—*Martina?*"

Tina nodded, then managed to answer, "Yeah."

"I can't believe—what is it?—it's you—I don't know what to—" muttered her father as he stood in disbelief. He stepped forward, gave her an awkward hug, then invited her inside.

"This is my wife—and Mindy," he said, as she saw mother and daughter staring back at her from across the room. "And this is . . . Martina." The little girl grinned shyly, but her mother looked at Tina with big eyes and no smile.

Mrs. Lockhart glared at her husband, then said, "C'mon, Mindy, you can help me in the kitchen." Mother and daughter left the room, leaving Tina alone with her father.

"Please—sit down," he said, gesturing toward the well-worn couch, whose torn cushions peeked out from beneath a mismatched bed sheet. He sat in a chair opposite her, paused, stared, then added, "I don't know what to say. I'm surprised to see you."

"Sorry about that. I guess I should have called first." She could hear the quaver in her voice.

"It doesn't matter. You're here now. But—well—why did you come?"

For ten minutes straight, Tina told him about the pain, the anger, the trying to forget. He said not a word, moved not a muscle. It felt like a dream. Someone was talking in her voice, describing what she had felt, using a tone that was slow and steady, with emotion, but no tears. The words conveyed feelings of the *past*, not the present. She didn't regurgitate the bitterness. She simply remembered it and told what she remembered.

Tina finished by telling her father about the baby announcement—how it had brought all her hidden feelings to the surface and that she could no longer live with her own secret. When she stopped talking, she looked at her dad. His lips were pursed, just like her own whenever she was trying not to cry. But still he said nothing. So she said what she most wanted to say—wasn't sure she *could* say.

"I didn't come to hear you say you're sorry. I came to tell you that I'm sorry for hating you. I'm sorry for pretending that you didn't exist. I came to say . . . please forgive me."

He sat and stared at her, his eyes in a glassy trance. Then he seemed to notice that she had stopped talking. He rose slowly from his seat, stepped over, and gave her a hug. "I'm sorry," he whispered. It was more than she expected, and sweeter than she could have imagined.

Mrs. Lockhart interrupted. "Honey, there's a strange-looking Oriental boy sitting in front of the house. He's been there for a while. Maybe you should find out what he's doing here."

"That's my friend!" Tina gasped, realizing she had forgotten all about Matt, who truly was her friend now. "He came with me on the train."

"You took the *train*?" asked her dad. "That's clear across town."

"We took a cab the rest of the way." Tina looked at her watch. "I better go. We've got to catch the last train back."

"Let me drive you," offered her father.

"Honey, how can you?" said Mrs. Lockhart, looking upset. "You're working graveyard tonight!"

"At least let me drive you to the train station." He grabbed his keys from the table next to the front door. Mrs. Lockhart walked out of the room without saying anything.

Outside, Tina introduced Matt to her father as they climbed into his car. It was old and rusty, like the cars they'd had when she was a kid. On the drive back to the station, her father asked her about school, her college plans, how her mom was. He seemed genuinely interested, but Tina felt a little uncomfortable talking about it. Up till now, she had been talking about the past. She wasn't quite sure how she felt about letting him into the present.

When they got to the station, Matt hopped out of the back seat and shut the door. Tina turned to her father to say thank you. He grabbed her hand. "I wish we had more time to talk. Can I see you again?"

"Yes. I think that would be good." She gave him a quick hug and climbed out the door.

34

The Gospel According to Matt

As they waited for the train, Tina felt a rush of panic as she thought for the first time about her mom, who would have gotten home by now and found no Tina, no note, nothing at all. Tina found a phone booth and made a collect call.

"Where are you, Tina? Are you okay?" Her mom sounded upset.

"I'm fine, Mom. I went to visit Dad."

"What?"

"It's okay. I'm fine, really. I took the train. I'm on my way back now." Tina tried to reassure her, but she could tell it wasn't working.

"You went alone? What's gotten into you, Tina?"

"I'm with a friend. I'm sorry this sounds so crazy, but really, it's all right. I'll tell you about it when I get home."

"You bet you will. Call me when you get to the station. I'll come and pick you up." Her mom spoke in short choppy sentences whenever she was angry.

"Please don't be mad at me. It was something I had to do. You'll understand when I tell you."

"I doubt *that*," her mother replied, a little less harshly. "We'll see. But are you sure you're all right? Is Amanda with you?"

"No, I'm with a friend from school. He's watching out for me," she added, as she saw Matt pointing toward the tracks. "You can meet him when we get there. The train's here, I've got to go. And Mom, I love you."

"I love you too, dear. Call me when you arrive."

Safe on the train heading homeward, Tina felt lighter than air. She hadn't fully known the awful weight of her feelings for her dad till that weight had begun to lift last night. Now the last pound was gone. She was soaring.

She had no idea what would happen with her dad—when she'd see him again, what they'd talk about, if the bad memories would flood upon her again.

Could she ever know in her heart that she had forgiven him?

There was a world of possibilities, both hopeful and frightful—yet tonight, she didn't worry. She felt she could handle anything.

Most of all, she felt like she could stop worrying about herself. For the past two weeks, she had been thinking mostly of her own life—how to act, how she appeared to others, and this week, how she had been so selfish in the past. But even that last, painful soul-searching had ultimately been about *her*. Now, for the first time since she could remember, she felt free to *be* herself—free to stop worrying about "me" and focus on "others."

The first "other" she thought of was Matt. He had given up his whole afternoon and evening to help someone he hardly knew. He was a true servant—more like Jesus in that way than most of her Christian friends. And after thinking it, she said it, thanking him for his support, his friendship, his willingness to act like Jesus just when she needed Jesus the most.

Matt studied his fellow passenger, scrunched up into a ball on her seat, chin resting on knees, a subtle smile peeking out even in her sleep. She had been like that for at least half an hour. Her last words had been to thank him for helping her, serving her, "for acting like Jesus for her."

He had returned her gushing appreciation with an embarrassed shrug. He had always been uncomfortable in accepting compliments. It was bad enough when the praise fit him. *But Tina compared me to Jesus.*

He was nothing like Jesus. He had gone with her merely for the adventure of it all. When she had burst out of Veras's class to tell him her wild idea, he'd thought it was crazy and exciting—something a rebel would do. He wasn't really doing it to help her; he'd done it to be—well—*different.*

If anyone had acted like Jesus, it was *Tina.* She had asked that question—What would Jesus do?— and then done it, even though it meant doing what seemed impossible. She hadn't told him what had happened inside the house. But he knew that whatever it was, it was exactly what Jesus would have done. She was as happy as anyone he'd ever seen.

More than that, she seemed at peace. She may have been happy about how things had turned out, but there was another happiness—a quiet joy seeping through, from the *inside out*. She didn't just *act* like Jesus. It was like she *was* Jesus—as if Jesus' personality had *possessed* her.

The truth of their differences hit him as the train pulled into the station. Try all he wanted to act like Jesus on the outside, it was still just a *costume*—something he could take on and off whenever it suited him. But Tina wasn't wearing a costume. From the inside out, she was *real*. A real Christian.

35

Reporting on Jesus

When Tina completed the quiz on the Christianity chapter, she noticed the quiet—just rustling paper, a pen tapping on someone's teeth, the sleeve of Camille's nylon jacket rubbing the desktop. And the sound of her own pulse pounding in her ears.

Tina knew what she would say in her report—she just didn't know how the class would react. And what would *Matt* say? She hadn't seen him at school all day—until he'd slipped into Veras's class just before the tardy bell, looking nervous and unsure. What was he thinking about all that had happened yesterday?

"Well, it's time!" announced Ms. Veras after she had collected the quizzes. "Time to hear from our two experimenters—our guinea pigs who volunteered to see what happens when you make decisions according to what Jesus would do. Who would like to go first?"

Tina raised her hand, gathered her notes, and stepped to the front of the class. Before starting, she looked around the room. Her Christian friends were smiling; Mitch was grinning from ear to ear. Matt was looking down, his long hair blocking his expression. Ms. Veras was sitting at her desk, notepad in hand.

"Ms. Veras, you were right. Trying to do what Jesus would do *did* make me miserable."

When she heard her name, Ms. Veras gave Tina a curious smile and planted her elbows on the desk, listening more intently.

"At first I thought it would be an easy assignment—I could just act like I always did, maybe a little bit nicer. But then *Mitch* here—" she said, pointing to him not unkindly, "—Mitch blabbed about the experiment at our church youth group. A few of them actually asked me if they could join—not for credit, just to do it on their own.

"For the past two weeks, I've watched that small group of people grow. And I've grown by watching them. Each of them showed me by their actions what it looked like to act like Jesus. They put me to shame. I was caught up in acting like a Christian. They were determined to act like Jesus. Before, I had thought those two were the same thing. Boy, was I wrong. As a *Christian*—or what I had always thought was a Christian—I could be the same old me: selfish, arrogant, pretending I had it all together, that I was better than other people. But when I tried to really do what Jesus would do— that was something else entirely. I couldn't be the same old me and act like Jesus at the same time. So I've been trying to abandon my old ways—to really do what Jesus would do, no matter what. And that's been a total pain in the butt."

The class laughed at her language—a welcome relief to the building tension.

Tina took a deep breath and continued. "Yesterday, I did the hardest thing I've ever done. I went to see my father, whom I hadn't seen in four years. He abandoned my mom and me and I hated him for it. As a Christian, I had managed for years to keep hating him—and to justify it. After all, he deserved it. But when I asked, 'What would Jesus do?' I hated the answer even more. Because Jesus didn't practice hatred. He practiced forgiveness. And that seemed impossible.

"But somehow, I managed to do the impossible— at least part of it, anyway. It was awful and scary— and if a friend hadn't helped me, I never would have made it." She looked at Matt; he had his head up now, and he smiled back at her as she continued. "When I saw my father, I told him that I was sorry for hating him. It wasn't some magic moment like you see in the movies. And it didn't suddenly make everything he did okay. But that's something he has to live with. The hatred was something I couldn't live with any longer—not after this experiment.

"Anyway, like I said, that is just *part* of what Jesus would do. The next part is scarier. Because to really do what Jesus would do, I will have to forgive my father. I really wanted to stand up here and tell you that I've done that—that I've done what Jesus would do, even in the hardest thing I've ever had to face. But I'm not there yet. It's clear to me that that's going to take a while. It's also clear to me that it's *not* impossible. If Jesus can guide me through everything I've faced in the past two weeks, he can guide me the rest of the way. Because if Jesus can forgive me for all the hateful, selfish things I've done to him, he can help me forgive others for doing the same to me."

Tina sighed in relief—the tough part was over. With tears in her eyes and something close to laughter in her voice, she finished her report. "So yes, Ms. Veras. Doing what Jesus would do—all the time, every time—that's impossible. He was perfect, and I'm far from it. And yes, it made me miserable. But it was my own misery—caused by my own disobedience to him. The *joy* I feel right now, from doing what Jesus would do with my father—that comes straight from Jesus."

As she walked back to her desk, the class was quiet. Ms. Veras broke the silence with her applause. Then the class erupted. When she sat down, Camille reached over and grabbed her arm. Tina looked up; Camille's cheeks were wet, but her smile was broad.

"Thank you, Tina," Ms. Veras said when the applause had faded. "For your honesty—and for your humility."

Tina turned to see her teacher smiling at her. She returned the expression—the first smile she'd given Ms. Veras in many days. Ms. Veras scribbled something on her notepad—Tina's evaluation, no doubt.

"OK, Mr. Chen, let's hear from you."

Tina watched him as he made the long walk from his desk at the back of the room. He was wearing his trademark army jacket, his shirt untucked, and his hair as messy as ever. When he turned to face the class she noticed how tired he looked—his eyes were dark and red, his mouth in an unchanging scowl. *Please, God,* she prayed, *whatever he says, help him get through it.*

Matt Chen pulled a crumpled sheet from his coat pocket and began: "Here's the opening to my speech. *If being a Christian means doing what Jesus would do, then I'm a Christian. And by the way, I'm an atheist.*"

A few of the students laughed. Tina cringed.

Matt refolded the paper and stuffed it back in his pocket. "I wrote that two weeks ago. You're probably wondering what an atheist is doing taking part in an assignment about Jesus. To be honest, I volunteered because I wanted to prove that Christianity was a joke. How could anyone base their whole life on what somebody who lived two thousand years ago supposedly did and said? I figured I could just read some of the religious stories, do what they said, and prove that anyone could do the same thing—even an atheist. Plus, I needed the extra credit."

Most of the class laughed at that one—a nervous laughter, the kind that comes after a scary scene in a movie.

"So I guess in one way," Matt continued, "I was like Tina. I thought this would be easy. Some of it was. As I read the stories about Jesus, I found something really cool: Jesus was a total rebel. He was always doing things that ticked people off. He'd spend time with the wrong people, get yelled at by all these religious people, then tell them to shut up. He cared about the homeless, people who were handicapped, people everyone else looked down on. In a lot of ways, he was kind of like an Antee."

"Yeah, right!" someone muttered. Someone else laughed. Tina watched for Matt's reaction. He stumbled at the comment, but quickly recovered.

"But most of all, Jesus made people think. About what they were doing, how they were acting, how they treated others. And that's what he did for me. He made me think about my life. And the more I thought about my life, the more I realized I was pretty messed up. I get mad when people rip on me because of how I dress, or because of the people I hang out with. But then I do the same to Christians, making fun of who they are. I thought I was a pretty honest guy, but when I saw how Jesus was, I realized I lie all the time. I'm proud of myself because I'm not racist—I hang out with people of all colors. But when my parents start speaking Chinese to each other in public, I'm embarrassed. I'm ashamed of being a minority.

"Asking that question about what Jesus would do has forced me to see how much of a hypocrite I am. Jesus always did the right thing, in every situation, even when it got him into trouble. I just do what gets me into trouble, whether it's right or not. I thought that's what it meant to be a rebel."

He paused to look around the room, and seemed to lose confidence when he did. Then he looked at Tina. She smiled back at him, trying desperately to cheer him on with her look.

He kept his eyes on her as he started again. "But I met a Christian who showed me the difference. Being a rebel doesn't mean breaking the rules. It means obeying a *different* set of rules. And sometimes when you do that, you make people mad. That's how Jesus was. He didn't break the rules to make people mad. He just obeyed God's rules, and some people didn't like it. He obeyed God in *everything* and even got himself killed for doing it."

Matt stopped again. The class was dead silent. He looked over at Ms. Veras. "That's when I realized that there was just no way I could do this assignment. To do what Jesus would do, I would have to obey *God*, just like he did. I would have to *love* God, just like he did. I would have to *believe* in God, just like he did. You can't just act like Jesus in some ways, but not in others. You can't just pick and choose. You either accept the whole Jesus, or none of him. He was either right or totally wrong. I believe he was right. I believe that if I did try to act like him in every way, my life would be better."

He paused and looked straight at Tina. "I believe in Jesus."

Tina was stunned. She didn't think to applaud till Matt was halfway to his desk. Apparently, the rest of the class was even more shocked—it was she who broke their trance. Most of her classmates joined her, but some just shook their heads.

Ms. Veras thanked Matt for his "surprising report," then gave the weekend reading assignment over the groans of the students. When the bell rang, the teacher dropped Tina's report evaluation on her desk, then hurried back to give Matt his before he slipped out the door.

Tina looked at her evaluation, grabbed her books and ran from the room, excusing herself from Camille and Mitch and a few of the others who were trying to congratulate her.

When she caught up with Matt, she threw her arms around him, too overwhelmed to utter a word. When she let go, Matt showed her his evaluation, pointing to the note Ms. Veras had written at the bottom. Tina read it—and then looked back up at

Matt and laughed, with such a rich and deep and heartfelt laughter that she felt as if she might just totally lose it right there in the hallway.

Ms. Veras had written the same note on both reports:

> "Well done, good and faithful servant!
> You have been faithful with a few things;
> I will put you in charge of many things.
> Come and share your master's happiness!"

—my favorite verse
Ms. Veras

We want to hear from you.
Please send your comments about this book
to us in care of the address below. Thank you.

ZondervanPublishingHouse
Grand Rapids, Michigan 49530
http://www.zondervan.com